Daughter of God and Man

By

Albert Ruggiero

Chapter 1

To Tame the Day

Abigail Wilson refused to let this day be like any other. It had to be a time filled with answered questions about the past and the future. She wouldn't let it end until she made these sunlight hours answer for their existence.

She ran out to the half plowed field were Noah was tilling the grassland. She was desperate. Her shoes dug deep into the virgin soil as she tried to catch Noah. She finally slowed him down when she grabbed his arm and he was surprised, but more than that, she detected in his body language his annoyance as he raised his eyebrows and gave her a glassy stare while he plowed the field. She smelled the fresh earthy aroma of the black life giving soil coiled up behind the blade.

"Where are my mother and Father buried," she shouted as she tried to keep up with him as he plowed. Her legs ached because she was carrying her weight for two now as the baby in her womb shifted from side to side. She pressed her hands even harder into his arm and stared deep into his eyes for the answer. His forearm was muscular.

His frustration welled up in his gut as he pulled off the reins from the back of his neck and stopped. He rested the reins on the wooden plow, and then leaned on it for support. "You never asked me about your parents before." After that he rolled up both his sleeves. She could see that he was also leaning on the plow for emotional help. He let out a long sigh. "Okay, what it is?"

"It was only just since Lawrence came back from the war that I learned that I was adopted," She said. She shook his arm hard wanting an answer right away and stared into his eyes. A desperate scared feeling rose up from her gut. She was so afraid that her questions would not be answered.

He looked down at her. "Aren't you happy here on the farm?"

She could see that he was sad and for the first time she saw tears welling up in his light brown eyes. The same stare that she saw in the cows eyes as it was being milked.

Everything about Noah reminded her of the farm. He was a farmer and that's all he was and he was only willing to give anything of value to anybody, even information, if it didn't interfere with the workings of the farm.

"No, no you don't understand," she said. She little by little let go of his arm and pressed with loving affection on her pregnant round belly. It felt good and scary at the same time and her stomach was hard and growing. Deep inside she felt what she could only describe as the fluttering of butterflies. Every day the thing inside of her was becoming part of her. She was growing it, nurturing it, bringing it into the world.

"What don't I understand?" He leaned back on the plow and crossed his arms in front of his chest. The plow settled down into the black rich soil.

She pointed towards the road. "Everybody is leaving me. In my whole life I couldn't hold on to anybody long enough to make a real connection except for Lawrence and now he's gone. He left because he said he had to find out who he was. Don't I have the same right to find out who I am and where I came from?" She grabbed her chest in breathless anticipation of his answer.

Noah unclasped his arms, grabbed her, and pulled her close to his chest. "Yes you do have a right ta find out who you are," he said. "Now go back to the edge of the field and sit and wait for me. We'll talk about it after I get done plowin' this pasture."

He smelled sweaty and masculine.

She walked back towards the edge of the field and when she looked up she saw the black Turkey vultures that Lawrence had told her about. A cold shiver ran up her spine. He said they traveled behind the troops and after the battle they would swoop down and eat the dead soldiers in the fields. She didn't want to be like one of those soldiers just skin and bones, just a memory.

She trembled, as she sat down on a peach basket and gazed into the meadow. Daniel walked up behind her through the woods, with a torch in his hand. "Hello miss Abigail. We is preparing the field to go to sleep," he said. She got a whiff of the resinous aroma of soil and the fresh odor of cut green grass coming off of his body and heard the pop of the flame from the torch as it consumed the wooden stick.

Meanwhile Noah had brought rebel and the plow back to the edge of the forest and grabbed another torch touching it to Daniel's flame. The flame smelled like charcoal as it consumed the stick.

The field was going to be left fallow, which was the reason that Noah plowed around the edges, two plow widths deep. That would be the safety zone so that when he burned the fields the burn wouldn't get away and scorch the forest. The strips of soil coming off the bottom of the plow looked like dark layers of chocolate cake batter.

Daniel trudged over the thick black plowed dirt and into the high grass, still with the torch held high above his head. He struggled to walk through the soil as if he were walking through the snow. It took him five minutes to get to the other end of the long narrow field. Noah was on the opposite side. "Okay Danny," Noah hollered. "Touch her off." Then both men poked and waved their burning torches into the dry grass in front of them.

The fire consumed the thirsty grass on both sides of the field while white billowing smoke rose into the sky. Abigail grabbed her skirt and pressed it close to her nose, and peered out over it, protecting her breath from the noxious fumes. The smoky tang of the bacon she had that morning wafted up her nose because the smell of the pork was still on her apron.

To Daniel and Noah this routine was just a way of preparing the fields but she saw it in a different way. It was as if the burning of the field represented the burning of her past life, the life with Lawrence, the life in anticipation of being taken care of. That was all burned away.

Now, it was her turn to find out who she was and where she came from. She felt it was her right to know the unknowable. Even though the flames were hot against her face she smiled under her protective shroud because she was feeling the growing of a new life inside her belly and the anticipation of seeing a page in the book of her life turned over to reveal secrets that had been buried.

Noah walked through the furrowed ground and then stood on her left side. He had a hanky tied around his nose and mouth. He took the torch and pushed the burning top of it into the cold black soil so it sizzled and finally went out. "As soon as da fire is out we'll go and see where your parents are buried," he said as he leaned the torch on a nearby oak tree and then reached to the back of his neck and untied his handkerchief.

Both Noah and Daniel looked like bandits with the handkerchiefs over their faces.

"All this time you knew where they were buried and never told me about it, why?" Her question was muffled under her apron. She dropped her shroud and looked up at Noah while she narrowed her eyes. There was tightness in her chest.

"Would it have made any difference?" He stared back into the field.

She pushed herself with her feet around the peach basket, still sitting, until she faced him. The basket crackled. But as she dug for an answer in the deepest part of her mind she realized from the bottom of her heart that he was right.

She just looked up at his profile because he was still looking at the burning field and then said; "No, I guess not." She looked into the flames just as Noah was doing and there were no answers there either.

Daniel joined them and all three stood there watching until the grass was nothing more than a smoldering pile of ash. His hanky was still around his throat.

"Daniel, unhitch rebel from the plow and go get the buckboard, we're goin' into town," Noah said. No words were said while they waited for the buckboard. The silence between Noah and Abigail went on with both of them staring at nothing for the time they waited for Daniel to bring up the wagon.

In a little while Daniel returned with the carriage; Noah and Abigail walked through the field and to the carriage and got on. The spring seat squeaked as Noah snapped the reins over the rump of the horse. Daniel rode in the back.

What should I call him now that I know he's not my flesh and blood? Who is this man sitting next to me now? Is he my father? Is he my guardian? Who is he? She thought.

Chapter 2

The Graves Talk to Abigail

By now it was getting dark and there was no moon to see their way down the road. "Don't you think it would be better if we did this in the morning Abby?" Noah asked.

"No, after all these years I want to find out now. I have to know where they're buried." She looked into the dark woods searching for a sign of light.

"Okay Abby." Noah slapped the reins harder over the back of the horse so that it trotted down the road faster. "It's too dark, can hardly see the road. Daniel, go in front of da wagon with a lantern and light the way."

After Noah stopped the wagon, Daniel lit the oil lamp, went around to the front of the buckboard and grabbed rebel by his bridle. They were just a dot of light traveling through inky darkness. Beyond the glow, the forest stood guard over shadows of the night cast by their shimmering lantern. Abigail was never afraid of the darkness until that night. Every tree, every bush, every shadow was her enemy to be feared. She inched closer to Noah so that she could feel his arm pressed against her arm. Even though she had doubts about who Noah was, she felt better sensing the touch of another human being.

At last they reached Packardville Road Cemetery, in front of them was a small burial ground set back from the road, buried into the woods. The lamp flickered off of ghoulish trees, and danced through the woods. The entrance of the graveyard was neglected with overgrown brambles over the paths that led to the graves.

The shadows assaulted her imagination. The trees alive and moving, stared down at her, grave stones shifted and danced in glimmering light. But the most disturbing sight was the stone mausoleum with its heavy blocks of stone over its door and the fact that it looked similar to their root cellar at home. Except behind its bulky oak door the possibility of dead bodies lying in coffins came to Abigail's fearful mind.

A small field stone fence flanked the little house on each side of the door. In back of the underground room the ground distended up so the grass looked like the fat belly of an old man. Stone walls and graves were moving and seemed to be coming alive.

"Welp, here we are," Noah said.

When Noah got off on his side of the buckboard, she scooted over and got down on the same side, and thrust her arm under his and held on tight.

"Where's we going?" Daniel asked as he moved closer to the little stone wall.

She had a sharp tone in her voice. "We're going to find my parents grave, Daniel."

His good judgment sensed her nervousness so he lifted the lantern higher above his head as he walked in front of them. They followed him, as they stepped up and over small stonewalls and then walked into the burial ground. The barbed blackberry bushes tugged at their garments and ripped away when they let loose from their clothes.

The stone grave markers were varied and appropriate for the cemetery; some graves had obelisk-type headstones towering over them, while one marker, a replica of a Roman urn, was covered with a shroud. Still another was a sculpted stone of a broken column which signified a life cut short. They walked through, looking left and then right for her parent's grave markers.

They walked by flat graves that seemed to have grown out of the ground. There were names like Simeon Humphrey, Arnold Dodge, Mary and Isaac Goose, and John and Martha Kendall. Abigail tried to walk next to the burial places and not on top of them because she felt it was disrespectful to trample on a grave.

"Over here Daniel," Noah shouted. He was their guide through the world of the dead.

"I'm a comin' mista' Noah."

"Right here." Noah pointed at two flat, worn down gravestones. They leaned forward into the grass. It was as if he was bringing the dead back to life when he showed Daniel where the couple was buried. Noah was their Virgil through the land of the dead. But he did not understand the significance of this event in the grave yard, and thought it was just the hysterical demands of a spoiled child.

Daniel swung the lantern between the gravestones to shed light on two strangers buried in the graves.

"Ruth and Eric Armstrong. Is that them?" Abigail asked.

"Yes Abby."

She kneeled down in front of the headstones and pushed them up so they stood tall and straight. The headstones scraped along her fingers. Then she pulled away grass and sod from around them and brushed off dirt from the front of the stones. "Hi mom, hi pop, it's me Abby your daughter, come to visit you."

"Daniel, what's the matter?" Noah asked.

The metal pinged when he shook the lantern and the glass clinked against the sides. "No more fuel mista' Noah." The lantern flickered so he shook it again, hoping that the light would last just a little bit longer. The handle on the lantern jingled. Despite glowing bright one last time it flickered out. They were left in the dark among graves, poplars, and pines.

They were blind. They stood still; arms outstretched groping through the cemetery. Abigail toppled over headstones of many of the dead people's graves. Then, little by little as if by magic, her eyes became accustomed to the darkness. It was as if the night had stolen just enough light from the stars to allow them to see.

"Come on Abby," Noah said as he grabbed her arm and escorted her through the graveyard. He was the sorcerer that knew the way out of the world of the dead and into the world of the living. With a great deal of care, he helped her step over the little stone wall and then down onto the ground.

The sound of the three explorers' as they shuffled through the crisp leaves fell on deaf ears.

She wondered if her parents had heard her saying hello to them while they rested side by side.

They groped their way back to the buckboard with Noah's help, and with Daniel following close behind.

Rebel's ears pricked forward and he pawed the ground in his eagerness to leave the dark forest. Noah reined the horse to the side of the road and turned him back away from the grave yard. They were headed home. But Abigail turned and looked back, straining to see her parent's graves. She lifted her shoulders and took in a deep satisfied breath. "Now I know where they are," she said to Noah.

"Do you feel better?" Noah asked.

"Yes."

Chapter3

Her Friends Welcome Her

While they rode down the road they saw little glimmering lamp lights coming from farms on the hill. But in front of them the road was shadowy, so they moved slow and careful.

When they finally got home, both Noah and Daniel lit the lanterns. They all sat in the summer kitchen drinking coffee.

"I'm glad that you found your parent's resting site Abby," Noah said. He reached out and touched her hand.

"I am too Noah," she said as she sipped a little coffee.

He put the coffee cup up to his lips, about to take a sip, when all at once, he stopped. He rubbed the back of his neck and then looked up at Abigail. His brow was furrowed. "You're calling me Noah now?" He set his cup down and stared at her. The cup clinked in the saucer.

"Yes, I think it's more appropriate, don't you?"

"No. Your parents won't turn over in their graves if you still call me Pa."

With a soft expression on her face she reached over and touched his hand. "Okay Pa it's a deal."

There was a long silence and then all of a sudden Daniel spoke up. "Me and my sista don't have no parents. Don't know where they is at. Don't even know if they is still alive."

"Sorry to hear that, Daniel," Abigail said. She looked over at him with a sad smile.

"My sista writes me from a place called Fitch's Home for Soldiers in Noroton Heights. She helps with the kids that's there."

"What does she do there?"

"Oh…she helps the teacher with keepin the kids quiet and paying attention to their books."

It was as if a spirit had grabbed a hold of Abigail and was in her head bringing her to a realization that made her out-and-out joyful. Her color became flushed and a grin formed across her face. She tipped her head back and turned her face to the sky. "The kids, the soldiers. Teach, teach, teach," she shouted. Then she got up and hugged Daniel. "Thank you Danny. You saved my life."

"My pleasure miss Abigail." He turned to Noah and shrugged his shoulders.

Abigail all at once ran outside and began to twirl around with arms out stretched and her face pointed into the sky. Her shadow, illuminated by the porch light, spun with her; first it slid over the house, and then dropped to the ground, then skirted over the roof of the barn and finally came to rest at her feet.

Noah ran after her. "Abigail what's the matter with you?" he asked. "You act like you're possessed."

She skidded to a stop. "I am Pa. Thanks to Daniel; I know what I want to do." She grabbed Noah's arms, wanting to share her joy with him. "I want to be a teacher. A teacher just like I taught Lawrence, a teacher to little kids and broken soldiers."

Knives came from Noah's mouth and stuck in her heart when he said; "You can't. You have to stay here and help with the farm." Then he turned and walked away not saying another word as he went into the barn.

Abigail stood frozen in place just staring in the direction of the shed. Her smile and the joy that had come to her face melted away and dripped down onto the earth. As she watched him walk away, she lowered her shoulders and stared at the ground. At that instant she became aware of the fact that there was nothing she could do to change her situation. She was as much a slave as Daniel was. She had no money, she had no power to change her position, and above all she couldn't change the fact that she was a woman.

After the encounter with Noah she had to get away to rebuild her soul, some place that was her special place where the earth fed her hope. But first she had to get some food for her friends.

As it happened, the speed that she had going into the kitchen startled Daniel so much that he spilled his coffee in his lap as he watched her run back out again. It was a quick visit to get some left over bread and then she was off. The new formed baby in her womb got jostled and it felt like a flock of little sparrows in her belly, but it was too important a quest for her to worry about that. She had to feed her soul in a hurry before she lost it. It was as if the baby was as light as a feather as she ran through the woods.

There was a space that she traveled to, to make her soul feel free and connect with other wild living things. She felt so alone and rejected in the human world. She went through the corn field next to the house, pushing plants aside in the dark as she headed for the cove hidden in the stream under a drooping willow tree. The corn stalks protested as they crackled and whooshed while she slid through them.

This secret place was her sanctuary surrounded not only by willows but also white birch and lush strong oak and hickory trees. Her scent became that of a woodland creature so that she blended into the forest as she left the odor of the human world behind.

Abigail whistled and three river otters came out from behind a mound of dirt. They all sat up on their hind legs for a second, sniffing the air, bobbing up and down, and twitching their bodies back and forth in an effort to get as much sensory information from the intruder and the environment that they could. At last they settled down because they recognized the image and smell of their friend.

Abigail tossed the left over bread at the otters. They picked it up, and with their little hands began to wash the food off in the stream. They clicked and clacked at each other as they ate their fill. Then they began to play by sliding down a makeshift drop that they had fashioned out of the clay bank next to the stream. She smiled to watch such happiness. The human world dissolved away.

Chapter 4

A Hard Deal is Struck

Maybe it was her dissatisfaction with the boring chores that she had to do, or maybe her feeling that she belonged somewhere else and was unable to go there, which made Abigail neglect her chores; washing clothes, washing dishes, dusting and washing the windows, gathering water from the well, sewing and knitting, milking the cow, and gathering the eggs for breakfast. The clothes sat in the tub still wet, dishes were piled up in the sink, and windows were caked with dust, cows became bloated with milk, and eggs piled up in the chicken coop until the chickens stopped laying and began to peck at eggs on their nests.

But when all was said and done, the thing that really showed how Abigail felt about her chores was that she stopped dipping candles. The kerosene lamps were used, although Noah, being the frugal farmer that he was, wanted the candles to light the house. In point of fact, Abigail refused to shed any light into a house that kept her prisoner and a slave.

Abigail sat in the root cellar one afternoon reading the Iliad by Homer when suddenly Noah slammed through the door. "What the blazes are you doin.'"

Abigail startled, looked up at him as he stood on the top of the stairs to the cellar with his fists clenched by his sides. "I don't know what you're talking about Noah. I'm just reading," she said, just as she put the half open book on a small chair next to her.

"Nothing is done, or just half done." He walked down a few steps and leaned his back against the jam to the door, folded his arms in front of him, and then stared at Abigail. "You're reading and not paying attention to your chores. Do you want to be one the characters in your book?"

She looked at the book sitting on the chair and then looked up at Noah. "Yes I would."

"Well, you can't. You're not a princess you're just a farm girl on a one-hundred and eighty nine acre farm and you have to pull your own weight. The vegetables are rotting in the baskets and the feathers in the feather beds have to be washed in suds so they don't smell anymore.

"I feel like a prisoner." She picked up the book and slammed it shut then stared into the nothingness of the root cellar. Her eyes filled up with tears.

"And I want you to stop drinking the rum that you're supposed to use for washing your hair. Let me expl—"

"I get it," she said. She turned to face him. "I'll make you a deal."

By now he had calmed down a bit and was willing to listen. He sat down on the top step with his elbows resting on his knees and let out a long sigh. "Okay, what is it?"

"I'll work until the end of October or the beginning of November, or until we see the first snow flakes. And I'll work hard, just as I always have. But after that I want to go."

"Okay, it's a deal."

He got up and went to shake her hand to seal the contract. It was as if he was closing a business deal with a perfect stranger. Abigail shook his hand, with a frown on her face. Her hand hung limply in Noah's grip because now she became conscious of the fact that she was just a common laborer and not his daughter.

They both left the root cellar and walked up to the house but Noah peeled off and went into the barn and came out with something in his hand that Abigail could only see as a piece of metal. When he got down to the root cellar, she recognized what was in his hand as a rusted flat metal lock. He threaded it through the little metal eyelet on the door and into the eyelet on the wall of the little house and snapped it shut. Then he flipped the pad lock with his fingers so that it swung back and forth before he walked back up to the house. He had a slight satisfied grin on his face as he walked by her and into the summer kitchen.

Chapter 5

An Ally Comes to the Farm

It was past noon time and Abigail's schedule was to get sandwiches and beer for the men. She walked into the summer kitchen expecting to see Noah but he was gone. She staggered on her feet as if in a trance, her heart was heavy. For a second all she leaned on the sink with the palms of her hands, bowing her head as she sobbed. Suddenly she picked her head up and straightened out her shoulders. She never felt this way before. She was always happy and excited about life and she was determined to stay that way.

"I won't let him get the best of me," she whispered to herself. Then she got the cold chicken from the ice box and sliced off the meat from its breast, rested the bread on her belly and cut off four slices for the sandwiches. She stacked the slabs of bread and meat together with a tomato and put the sandwiches in a basket with two containers of bear next to them.

Abigail went out to the field of corn that was right next to the house. It was a late planted field that Noah hoped would yield corn into the fall season, so the corn was about chest high when Abigail walked through it. "Noah… Daniel…where are you?"

"Over here miss Abigail. I is right here," Daniel said.

She pushed aside the green stalks with her basket until she came to Daniel picking off some of the dead corn cobs. "Here you go Daniel. Good strong beer and chicken sandwiches."

"Thank you Miss Abigail."

She moved closer to him and with a steady, low pitched voice said; "Daniel would you do me a favor."

"Yes ma'am, whatever you want."

"Call me Miss Armstrong," she asked.

" Why, because that was your parent's name?"

"Yes," she said. "Where is Mr. Wilson?"

There was a confused look on his face but after a while he realized who she was talking about. "He's gone to town. Said he'd be back before dark." He took a sandwich out of the basket taking a big bite and knocked back a long swig of bear.

After she saw that Daniel was taken care of, she went back up to the house. She leaned up against the Zink sink and began washing the dishes. They clinked against each other and smelled sweet from the soap flakes that she added to the hot water. She ran a brush and then a dish cloth over the plates and cups. This kind of work was usually done in the scullery by hired maids but now it fell to Abigail and she resented it. The last thing she did was to pour chloride of lime into the sink and then pour hot water over it so it would disinfect the drain.

"Hello, is anybody there?" A voice split the silence of the kitchen.

Abigail jumped and then turned abruptly towards the door. "Yes, what is It," she asked as she bent towards the door.

"I was told to tell Abigail that I was the hired hand and that she was to show me my room."

Abigail walked over to the squeaky door and pushed it open. "Come in."

"Thanks ma'am. Are you Abigail?" He asked while struggling with his duffle bag draped over his shoulder and the carpet bag in his left hand.

"Yes."

On his forage cap he had the Artillery Corps insignia, two crossed field guns. They were gold metal. He had droopy eyelids and thin lips. Abigail looked at him straight in the eyes. He was only as tall as her and slightly built. She smiled inside when she thought of him. Finally somebody else knows what it's like to live in a world of giants, she thought.

"Hi, my name is William Collins." He held out his hand, but she just stood there with her arms folded over her chest watching him wrestle with his belongings.

"This way."

He watched her as she walked through the kitchen, through the living room, and up the stairs. She stopped in front of the room that Burton had slept in. She watched him while he pulled and rearranged his bags up the narrow steps. Finally he reached the top landing.

"You'll be using this room," she said as she pointed to the rope bed next to the window.

"Thanks," he said. He flipped his duffel bag onto the rope bed. At the same moment, two books fell out onto the floor. They were "Journey to the Center of the Earth," and "From the Earth to the Moon."

As soon as she saw the books she knew this William Collins was a kindred spirit and Noah, unknowingly, had given her an ally in her battle to become her own person.

Without any hesitation she ran over and picked up one of the books cradling it in her hands. "From the Earth to the Moon," she said as she looked at the title. "Isn't that a crazy notion?"

"No, it isn't." He walked closer to bolster his point. "I was a connoneer during the war, and I can tell you some of those cannon balls went far. We had a 10-pounder Parrott cannon that shot a ball 1850 yards and another 12-pounder Whitworth that shot 2800 yards."

Still holding on to the book she turned and smiled and cocked her head. "Yes, but that's not as far as the moon, is it?"

"No, I guess not," he said. "But in that book they designed a cannon that could shoot a projectile to the moon."

"And where was this place that they had the cannon," she asked.

"Stone's Hill in Tampa Florida. They started the construction of the gun at 27° 7′ northern latitude and 5°7′ western latitude. They dug a circular hole 900 feet deep and 60 feet wide." he said. "Do you want to read it?"

Abigail raised her eyebrows and a small smile began to form on her lips as she looked at the cover of the book. When she started to give it back, she felt a sadness settling in her belly right next to the baby. "I can't read it; I'm too busy during the day."

"No, no, you can have it as long as you want. Take your time. You'll really enjoy it." He waved off the book indicating that he wanted her to keep it.

"Okay." When she took back the book, she gave it a place of honor, as she pressed it against her pregnant belly. The baby kicked for joy in her tummy. Then Abigail smiled at her new friend.

"I've got to leave now because I'm meeting Noah in the north pasture to get instructions. See ya." He went through the door, down the steps and out to the fields next to the house.

She was bound and determined to beat this sentence of servitude that had been imposed on her. She would not allow Noah to stop her from reading. Sometimes she would hide the book inside her corded petticoat, or close it quickly when she heard somebody coming and hide it under her apron.

Then, she got the brilliant idea to sew a pocket in the back of her Pinner apron that covered the front of her dress. That way she could pull the book out and read it any time she wanted.

All her life she was taught to be chaste, dutiful, and silent. She felt like a commodity, like a can of coffee or a basket of corn that could be bought and sold in the market.

My obedience and passivity in front of men is the only weapon I have. I let them think that I'm slow-witted and unaware of the world around me. We're owned by our husbands, or our father's, or our employers. Men trust other men, they don't trust women. The husbands should know that their wives have sense like they do. Women see and smell and have the ability to savor the sweet and sour of life, she thought.

All these thoughts ran through her head as she milked the cow and read at the same time. The cows were milked three times a day and this was the second time in the schedule. She squeezed the tits of the cow, watching the stream of creamy white life hit the bottom of the pail and heard it splash into the puddle of milk. She thought about feeding her baby the same way, with milk from her body. At the same time, she glanced at the open book next to the animal's right hoof.

From behind her she heard somebody shuffle into the barn. On the spur of the moment she kicked the book closed with the toe of her shoe and then with a rustle of dry hay, covered it over. She turned on her stool to face Noah.

"So what do you think of William?"

"He's sort of a half pint isn't he? He's knee high to a grass hopper."

"Yeah, he is short."

"He's okay I guess, but he's not Lawrence, he's just a farm hand like me." Then she turned back and continued to milk the cow. As is the case with a young pregnant girl, her hormones were going wild. She jumped up spilling the pail of milk as she turned to face Noah. "Why are you treating me so mean?" She could see that Noah was startled and surprised by her anger.

"I…ah don't know what you mean," he said. "We all have to pull our own weight. The chores have to be done."

"Well, this farm hand is tired and I'm going to take a break." She dashed out of the barn and got onto the buckboard which already had rebel harnessed to it. She snapped the whip next to his ear which made him lurch forward. She was off down the dirt road that led into the corn field. After a while, when she thought that she was far enough away, she pulled up on the reins to slow the horse down.

As the horse slowed down to a trot, she noticed William in the tomato patch. She pulled the wagon to a stop on the side of the road. He stood up and waved to her. "Hi Abigail. Nice to see you again." He walked over to her with a basket of tomatoes and placed them in the back of the wagon.

"Hi William."

"Call me Bill will ya," he said.

"Okay Bill."— She reached into the basket of Great White Beefsteak tomatoes and picked one out and handed it to him—"Take a bite. They're really sweet this time of year."

"Yeah, they sure are." The juice dripped down his chin. He laughed and then wiped his mouth on his sleeve. "I guess I should have brought a napkin."

"Can I have some?"

"Sure." He reached into the basket for another tomato.

"No," she said. "I want a taste of yours." Then she took it out of his hand, smiled, and bit into the same place that he had bitten into. I wonder if somebody had seen what I had just did, whether they would think that I was a hussy. Were all pregnant women as bold as I had become? Could it be because the baby was living off my body and that is why I want to devour everything I see, including William?

"Great isn't it?"

"Yes it is,"—she was bending over the seat on the wagon by now and letting the juice drip from the tomato onto the ground and laughing—"ambrosia."

"What are you saying?" he asked.

"Oh, ambrosia was the food of the gods. Its food that will make us immortal. Don't you want to be immortal?"

"I don't think I'd like seeing everybody I love die."

"Yes I understand. It's hard to see people leave."

"I have a present for you, meet me in the barn after supper and I'll give it to you," he said just before he turned and walked away.

"What is it? Tell me." She stood up on the seat of the buckboard and shouted to him as he disappeared into the cornfield.

After he disappeared she heard a voice echoing through the middle of the field. "You'll seeee."

The sun was drooped next to the horizon signaling the end of another day and the beginning of another night. The goddess Nyx will be taking over the farm now, Abigail thought as she looked at the red color of the horizon. Even Zeus feared Nyx because she was older than him and her kingdom was inevitable.

She reined the horse back onto the road in the direction of the farmhouse. All of a sudden she pulled rebel to a stop between a corn field and a field full of cucumbers. She slid off the seat and down onto the road with care because of the baby in her stomach. As fast as she could, she ran into the cucumber patch and pulled off a long green cucumber and then ran over to the corn field and ripped off an ear of corn, bit into it tearing off the kernels'. Then she snapped the cucumber in half, sniffing the fresh inside of the vegetable, just before she bit into the white juicy insides. But this only satisfied her immediate need.

She went over and got back into the buckboard and headed for the farm house. As soon as she got through the door she headed for the ice box, and like a ravenous animal, after putting the chicken on the table, pulled a leg off and devoured it, then sliced off pieces of the breast. She leaned over the half eaten fowl with a deep gratifying sigh, "Ah that was so good." All of a sudden the demon that had taken hold of her subsided and her eating binge ended as she fell on the floor.

A loose tooth fell out of her mouth and plopped on the floorboards. Her unpredictable hormones were kicking in and the calcium in her body was being used up by the thing growing in her belly. She sat there and sobbed hysterically and then began to laugh at herself because she realized how ridiculous it was.

She got up with slow cautious movements as if she had just run a marathon. After that she went into the living room and collapsed into the rocker that was next to the fireplace. It only took a few rocks in the chair to lull her asleep.

After a while something pinched her awake. The clock rang six times. "Oh no." she said, "I have to make something for supper." She got up quick, leaving the rocking chair swinging back and forth as she ran into the kitchen. A dread grabbed hold of her. "What do I make?"—she gazed downward, using her hair as a shield up against her eyes to block the reality that nothing had been made—"I'll make some soup. That's easy and quick."

She got an aluminum container of chicken broth from the ice box and dumped it into the pot. Then added one pound of bread crusts, two ounces of butter and beat the whole with a spoon. She kept it boiling till the bread and stock were well mixed. She seasoned it with salt. "There, that's good enough."

Chapter 6

Nightmare of a Young Chimney Sweep

The next minute Noah and William kicked the steps on the porch and scraped the bottom of their boots on the blade attached to the landing. They clomped into the summer kitchen. The chairs squealed when they pulled them out from under the table. Daniel was still out in the fields and would be coming to supper late.

Noah sat down on the seat hard, grabbed a napkin, slapped it out quick and tucked it under his chin. "Well, where's supper?" He had a fork in one hand and a knife in the other as he banged on the table.

Abigail walked over to the table with two bowls of soup in her hands and placed them in front of the two men, and then she hesitated and timidly backed away. Her hands trembled and she could hardly catch her breath as she watched them stare at the soup. She put her hand under her throat waiting to see what would happen.

"What's this," Noah shouted. "I want a real supper with meat and potatoes and vegetables." He stared at Abigail while she was backed up against the sink. "You're not doing your job young lady."

She broke into tears and ran out the door.

"I'll go see if I can help," William said as he got up from his chair.

"No. Sit down and eat your supper. She'll get over it."

While William sat down Noah went to the ice box and got a plate of left over ham. He dropped it onto the table in front of him. The ceramic plate slammed on the wooden table as the ham jumped up and then settled down onto the dish. "There, that's better."

As William watched Abigail run out the door his thoughts went back to the time that he was a young apprentice to a chimney sweep in New York. He understood her frustration because just like her he felt trapped and unhappy once. But now, here, he was content because he had gone through the darkness inside of the chimneys and had come out of them stronger than when he went in.

****

There were little black boys that I worked with and one of the kids was five years old just going on six. He was small enough to snake through the nine inch by fourteen inch chimneys. And I think that Diablo Mc Coy, the master chimney sweep bought him and the rest of the boys from an orphanage. I was to apprentice with him for seven years, and after that I could become a master chimney sweep. But the Negro boys were indentured servants and they had to stay and work as long as McCoy said.

But in my case I was homeless in New York and had needed a job. And because I was small enough to squeeze through the chimneys and scrape the insides to dislodge the soot, McCoy took me on as an apprentice.

The new chimneys in some of the newly constructed buildings in New York were often angular and narrow. Diablo tried to climb into a chimney one day that looked a little bit bigger than the usual ones and got stuck; "Get me out of here boys. I'm stuck. My legs is wedged against the walls." Two black boys and I were laughing so hard at Diablo, that we hardly had the strength to pull him up and out of the smokestack. "That's it. From now on it's you boys that goes down in those holes," he said as he brushed the soot off his jacket and pants. Then he sat on the peak of the roof and let out a long sigh. "Let's go down to the fireplace."

It was my turn to climb into the chimney and dislodge the soot. But first I had to do it naked. We called it "buffing it." There were four of us, and I was the oldest. I had done it before but I could never get over the embarrassment of being naked.

When I first started my knees and elbows got all scraped up, but Diablo fixed that. He had hardened up the skin on my knees and elbows by making me stand close to a hot fire and rubbing in strong brine using a brush. He did it every night for a week until the skin hardened. Then, when I went up the flue the deadened skin acted like a pad against all the turning and scraping I had to do. I felt like a caterpillar inside the chimney.

Diablo fixed a cloth over the fireplace. I pulled my cap down over my face and held a large flat brush over my head, and wedged myself diagonally in the flue. Using my back, elbows and knees, I shimmied up the flue like a large black worm.

I used the brush to dislodge loose soot, which fell over me and down to the bottom. And I used a scraper to dislodge the solid bits. The walls looked smooth and new. My chest filled with pride in a job well done. Even though it was a dirty, dangerous job, it was the only thing I knew how to do.

When I reached the top, taking a deep breath of fresh air, I all at once slid back down to the floor and into the soot pile. Then, it was my job to bag up the soot and carry it back to the master sweep's cart.

After I had put on my soot covered shirt and pants and my black boots I bagged up the grime from the skin of the flue and put it on the carriage. We sold the soot to the farmers for fertilizer. We never left a job without gathering up our black gold in sacks.

We were totally indebted to Diablo McCoy, and in return he taught us the craft and finer points of chimney sweeping. Although he gave us a second suit of clothes we seldom washed them, or for that matter, ourselves. After climbing out of the chimney I was as black as the black 'climbing boys' that I worked with.

Maybe once a week we would jump into the creek and get clean; "Here I'z come Billy," said Ulysses Jefferson. He had landed pretty near my head after he let go of the rope that was hanging off the branch of a tree, over the river. Nobody ever taught him how to swim so he sort of doggy paddled back to the shore.

I swam over next to him, grabbed his chin and turned his head towards me. "You better go soak in the river a bit more Ulysses your still black."

"No amount of soakin' is goin to take that off mista' Billy."

"Why?"

"Cause that's me that you see." We both started to laugh so hard that we blew bubbles in the water. I took a liking to Ulysses. He seemed so small and vulnerable to me, and I was convinced that he needed protection. The future would tell the tale of how right I was about his needing an older brother to look over him. He was only six and that was thought to be just the right age to train a boy.

We started the morning by roaming the streets hollering out; "Soot Oh, Sweep, clean your chimney." We did four or five chimneys a day. But the only one that got rich was the Master Sweep. We were never paid; he just fed us and gave us a roof over our heads and let us sleep on the coal sacks. This was known as "sleeping black."

Sometimes to make us climb up the chimneys faster McCoy, the master sweep, would light a small fire of straw or brimstone candle to encourage us to try harder or scramble up the chimney faster. And sometimes he would send a boy up behind an apprentice that he thought was moving too slow to prick pins into the soles of his feet or rear end.

All the boys had that done to them, more than once, including me. I always thought it was part of the job and accepted it. The other boys followed my lead and never complained.

When I thought of their names I always laughed. They were all named after Presidents. Whether they picked out their own names or their parents named them I never could find out. But I sure was in distinguished company. There was skinny Zachary Taylor, nervous Andrew Jackson, and of course little Ulysses Jefferson. I sometimes think Diablo McCoy bought those boys as a joke just because of their names.

Little Ulysses would often get stuck with his knees jammed up against his chin. The harder he struggled the tighter he became wedged in the chimney. We pulled him out with a rope many times. I worried about him and did my best to let him only go in the easier chimneys'.

"I'll tackle this one Diablo," I said. We stood in front of a large, tall, expensive red brick house with four narrow chimneys' on the roof.

"No," he said. "Put Ulysses in this one. There's a lot of angles to get through."

"Okay."

That dark day in June an incident happened that broke my heart. It was drizzling and was slippery on the tiles of the roof. We slipped twice, trying to reach the peak. We climbed to the top of the building and I tied a rope around his waist and lowered him down.

After going through the chimney he went to the second angle of the fireplace and found it from top to bottom filled with soot which had come down from the sides. I looked down the dark chimney and saw him struggle to get through, and then heard him grunt and groan and slip and slide against the walls of the smokestack. He tried to move back up the flue but he couldn't because the soot had become so compressed that it was like a solid wall above him. So he tried to turn against the sharp angle of the solid stone shaft but the sharp angle of the bricks dug into his shoulders and the back part of his head.

I could hear him claw at the inside of the flue like a trapped animal, trying to move, but he was completely stuck. He cried and moaned.

I squeezed my shoulders into the hole but it was too small for me to go down in it. "Take it easy Ulysses we'll get some help." My voice echoed down the dark hole.

I grabbed the inside of the chimney and leaned over the eaves. "Diablo get help. Ulysses is stuck. Get the brick-layer; we've got to get him out," I hollered. All the boys and McCoy scurried around on the ground with Andrew and Zackary running up the street. A few minutes later they came back with the policeman and the mason in tow. They pointed up towards the roof.

Ten minutes later the mason and I were chipping away at the bricks in the chimney. With our hammer and chisel we broke down the flue, hollering down to the ground to watch for falling bricks. We pulled the vent apart as fast as we could and finally reached Ulysses. But it was too late.

He was in a fetal position. He looked so small, all curled up and motionless. He had suffocated. His black stocking climbing cap was over his mug and when I took it off; his eyes stared lifeless into my face. I pushed his eyelids closed with the palm of my hand.

After that, my heart wasn't in my work so I left the employ of Diablo McCoy. Unlike the other boys that were indentured servants, I was free to leave as I pleased. After I wandered around for many years I finally enlisted in the

Army and learned artillery. Even now, I get nervous and jittery when I'm in a

closed room or inside for too long. I guess it's all those years of climbing inside

the chimneys that made me that way. I just want to see the sky and be out in the

air.

"Do you want any of that ham?" Noah asked.

"Oh."—William shook his head and came back to the present—"I was day

dreaming. No. I'm not that hungry; I think I'll take a walk in the fresh air and then

bed down for the rest of the night."

"Good idea. We got a lot of work to do tomorrow." With that Noah

continued eating while William went out the door.

The air was cold and fresh. The New England fall weather put life into his

lungs. He breathed it in, thankful that he had a job that got him away from the hot

city. He walked into the barn expecting to see Abigail. He searched the horse

stalls and then went over and grabbed onto the railing on the stairs that led up to

the loft, and hollered up into the eaves of the barn; "Abigail you up there?" The

silence was broken by the horse in the stall swishing the flies with its tail and

stamping its back leg onto the wooden floor.

Disappointed, He went out to the dirt road in front of the barn, chewing on

a sprig of hay and with his thumbs hooked in his jeans, he stared down the snaky

path until his eyes became blurred from the strain of looking into the dark. All of

a sudden a ghost image came into view. It moved up the road and it got larger and more distinct as it came closer to the barn. It was Abigail strolling towards the house. Her sky blue work dress and white apron came into view.

"Abigail," William shouted. He waved his arms over his head.

She stopped as if the sound of his voice froze her to the path. She all of a sudden quickened her step until she was in front of him. "Hi William." She sat down on a log next to the barn, and looked up at him. "What's going on?"

"Oh nothing. I was wondering if you were all right." He took the sprig of hay out of his mouth and flipped it in the dirt.

"Yes. I was visiting my friends," she said as she clapped her feet together and smiled to herself.

"Your friends?" He furrowed his brow and stared at her. Even though William found her peculiar, he also anticipated her strange and unexpected ways.

"Yes. The otters and the foxes and the deer and the—"

"Oh, I understand." There was a silence while they waited for one of them to say something, to pierce the quiet that had descended into their conversation.

"I almost forgot. I have something for you that I know you'll like"—he ran off into the house, into his room and grabbed a purple silk bag and his chimney sweep top hat—"here you go."

By the time he came back, Abigail was standing up. "What is it?"—she put the top hat on her head and then opened the silk bag—"it's a spy glass."

"It's so you can look at the moon. Pull it open and point it at the crescent moon." She pulled the telescope open to its full extent and looked through it.

"The book you gave me was interesting, but it almost read like an artillery manual," she said while looking through the telescope and almost losing her hat while looking up to the sky. "Oh William this is magnificent. There are mountains and valleys and craters and oceans. It's another world!"

"I know." He smiled and a warm satisfied feeling ran through his chest.

"Do you think there are people living up there?" She put the telescope aside for a second and then stared at him and he knew she was expecting an answer.

"I don't know." As they talked a meteor streaked through the sky. "I just saw a shooting star Abigail."

She set the telescope down on a bale of hay. Then she instantly turned toward him. "You have to make a wish. Hurry before the magic is gone."

"Okay." He looked up into the hay loft while he mouthed a secret request for good luck.

"No, no. That's not the way to make a wish. Let me show you." She looked into the dark night sky, closed her eyes and crossed her fingers and then put her fingers on each side of her temples.

"Do you think your wish will come true?"

"I don't know yet." She rested her arms by her side and looked with sad eyes at the night sky.

"What was your wish?"

"I'm not supposed to tell you, or else the wish won't come true."

"You can tell me. I won't tell anybody else. Your secret will be safe with me."

"It's not a secret; it's more like a request to the gods. I want to leave here and go and become a teacher." She went over and collapsed the spyglass and put it back in the purple bag.

"You can still look through the telescope," he said with anticipation.

But she just sat hard on the bale of hay and stared into the darkness and began to cry.

"My hope has been stolen by Noah." She sniffled. "I'm beginning to hate him. But I have so much that I owe him because he adopted me and took care of me all those years."

William's heart ached for her. He sat down and rested her head on his shoulder. He drew her nearer to his side. "It's okay Abigail. I'm your friend."

"I know." They sat there a long time until Abigail fell asleep. William placed her head on the bale of hay and lifted her legs up so she could rest better, and then he left.

Chapter 7

An Evil is Transplanted

The one hundred an eighty nine acre island of land was Noah's special magical place. Everything grew because he willed it to grow. Everything was under the umbrella of his protection.

And sometimes he thought that he had influence over the elements, the winds and the rain, the storms and the hail, all obeyed his whim, he thought.

Mean while Noah had finished his supper and had gone out to the field with a paper bag full of ham sandwiches and a container of cold beer. He strode through the aisles of corn with the smell of the green plants in his nostrils and the earthy aroma of the dust kicked up by his feet. The corn plant's arms rustled against his shoulders as he marched through the field.

This was his kingdom and everything and everybody were his servants. He imagined the corn plants leaning back to let him go by. The tomatoes ripened on the vine after he stepped over them and the apples hung from the trees suddenly ripened and turned red. This was Noah Wilson's realm and neither natures' forces nor the influence of any human being was going to destroy it.

"Daniel…Daniel where are you?"

"Right here mista' Noah," he shouted as he walked up the road between the fields of corn.

"Here, I brought you something to eat." He handed him the food and then they sat on a pile of logs that were stacked by the side of the road.

"Thanks." The rustle of the paper bag and the slosh of the beer in the container, the field crickets chirping and the tree frogs peeping, were the only sound that could be heard for a while. The smell of alcohol wafted Noah's way when Daniel popped open the container of beer. Then Noah demanded Daniel's attention. He got up and put his foot on the logs and leaned into Daniel's face.

Daniel looked up at Noah. "It's a nice night. I was dreaming about that piece of land you promised me last year. I was thinkin' what I could do with it. I ain't complained about any of the work you gives me."

"I know. You'll have that land soon enough," he said. "You wouldn't want to go back to gettin' beaten and starved again would you?"

"No sir. I knows my place mista' Noah."

"Then I want you to keep an eye on William an Abigail for me. Let me know about everything they do. Become invisible."

"How's that?" He asked with a puzzled look on his face.

"Just don't let them see you."

"Okay."

"I also want you to do me a favor right now," he said. "Go get the buckboard hitched up, put a couple of shovels and picks in the bed and drive it back here."

In the mean time Abigail had woken up and had gone up to bed.

While Daniel was gone Noah stared at the same crescent moon that Abigail had looked at, but in his case it was for the health of the farm. He knew from his father that the waxing phases of the moon signaled a fertile and wet month. And that the first quarter, known as the light of the moon, were considered good for planting above-ground crops, putting down sod, grafting trees, and the most important thing of all, it was a time for transplanting.

By the time Daniel arrived with the buckboard, the crescent moon was overhead. The dark midnight mood took over the farm now and every plant was asleep and not aware of what Noah was planning.

"Scoot over and let me drive," Noah said. He pushed Daniel to the other side of the seat and grabbed the reins. "Giddy-up." He snapped the straps three times over the rump of the horse. They were off down the dirt road in the direction of the stone wall in the north pasture.

"Mista' Noah where are we going?" Daniel asked holding onto the bouncing seat with both hands.

"You'll see. Just hold on."

While they headed into the dark woods the moon became covered by a wispy black cloud so that the light dimed and the landscape turned alien and unfamiliar. The more the wagon pushed on into the dark woods, the more it traveled to an unholy destination.

"Whoa Rebel." Noah pulled up the wagon next to the wall that they had buried Burton under, lo those many months ago.

"Why is we here?" Daniel stared at the ghostly figure of the wall. He knew all too well where they were and he shook with fear.

"Take it easy Daniel. We've got a little job to do here and then we're through." Noah got off the wagon, went to the bed and grabbed one of the shovels, walked over to the stone wall and stuck the blade of the shovel in the dirt and then rested his foot on the shovel and rested his hands on the wooden handle as he stared at the makeshift grave. "We're here to make things right."

"What do you mean?" Daniel asked as he got off the seat of the wagon.

"We have to undo what was done here. I have to get rid of this guilt that's buried here," he said. "This grave is something that I won't tolerate on my land anymore."

"But mista' Noah, why now?" Daniel stood perfectly still and stared at Noah.

He turned his head at a snail's pace toward Daniel, making sure that he understood. A sudden and unfamiliar pang of emotion came over him. "Lawrence is gone and Abby will be gone soon. This was their sin, and I went along with it, so now I'm changing that, and getting rid of this curse on my land. Besides that, it's a good time for transplanting.

"Yes sir."

"Come over here and help me dig up this body so we can get it out of here."

The two men tore the flat rocks off the wall; they threw them in a pile next to an old hickory tree. The clunk of the rocks echoed through the darkness along with the ping of the pick-axe, as the tree stared down at the broken bodies at his feet. While the stones lay there heaped on top of each other they whispered; 'we're not beautiful and symmetrical anymore. We're just common now like our field stone cousins in the woods. Look at us, we're shattered and chipped.'

The only thing Noah regretted was the destruction of the well crafted wall that he had built. The fact that Burton was buried under it was of little consequence.

The task was done, and Noah felt good inside that they had dug up the body and was going to bury it someplace else and not on his land. This black incident would never be thought of or remembered as long as it was on some other piece of land, he thought. But what he didn't realize was that there would be changes from nature that would change his plans and everybody else on the farm.

The body was already loaded into the back of the buckboard and Daniel and Noah were headed back to the barn when it started to rain. At first it was only a drizzle but as they got closer to the house it began to rain steadily and the wind whipped up. It had become a true Nor'easter. The wind and rain blew sideways and the trees tried to shake off the rain like a wet dog.

The roar of the rain on the roof of the barn made the men shout at each other. Noah yelled over the wailing of the storm outside, while he was giving his explicit instructions. "Daniel, I want you to stay in the barn and watch to make sure that nobody finds out that Burton is in the buckboard."

"Yes'm mista' Noah."

Noah, his chin buried in his chest fought against the wind and the pelting rain to get to the summer kitchen.

For the rest of the night Daniel stood guard over the dead body while Noah sat in the kitchen smoking his pipe and wondering what to do next. He fell asleep with his legs rested on top of the pine table and his pipe, embers long gone from the bowl, dying out.

He woke up after an hour of restless sleep. On the way to the barn he passed by a small stream next to the house and it had become an angry flood. By then, the rain had stopped but the rivers were swollen with brown colored water and their banks were collapsed into the boiling, undulating torrent below.

"Daniel, Wake up," Noah said as he shook him. "We've got to get this thing done. Hitch up the horse."

The jingle of the chains on the harness and the clunk of the horse's hoofs inside the barn told Noah that the wagon was being readied. Daniel swung open the barn doors while he led the horse outside.

Noah got up onto the squeaky seat and Daniel sat next to him. The horse, Rebel, was wet, with a coat of rain still clinging to his mane.

Noah turned to Daniel with the reins in his hands. He whispered to him afraid that what they were about to was unholy. "I don't know what we're going to do with this 'Jonah' but we have to get rid of him before his curse infects us all."

"Yep." Daniel tried to find a more comfortable spot on the seat by moving his rear end around.

They were headed for the Packardville Road cemetery. The horse, Rebel, pulled them in that direction, as the men realized too late that they were next to the burial fields. All of a sudden they saw a crowd of men milling around the cemetery.

A man in a slouch hat and gray rubber rain coat walked up to the wagon.

"What's going on," Noah asked.

"We're trying to save the people buried in the graveyard so they won't float away down the river." The river had overflowed its banks and was carrying some of the caskets downstream.

"Oh, okay," Noah said. After the grave digger had left he turned to Daniel. "It's time to transplant, not only the crops but any problems that we have. This is our chance to get rid of Burton."

"How?"

"You'll see." He reined the horse to the bank of the cemetery, out of sight of anybody. "Get out and help me drop the body on the edge of the river." Both of them lifted the decayed body out of the back of the buckboard and plopped it next to opened graves and tangled caskets. It had a rotted meat smell to it. "There, that should do it. We're rid of him at last."

Noah gave out a long sigh of relief as he snapped the reins over the horse's rump as they went down the road towards home.

"I don't understand mista' Noah," Daniel said as he held tight to the seat.

"Don't you see? They'll think he's one of the people washed up by the flood. There's no way they could trace him back to us."

"Oh, I see." A Mona Lisa smile formed on his lips.

The man in the moon looking down had seen what the two men in the buckboard had done. There was a frown on its crescent face as it peeked around its dark side to see what they had tried to hide in the dark.

And Noah thought that nobody could trace them to the body. He was satisfied that the problem was taken care of, and he had no regrets for doing what he had done, because he knew that the land was grateful that he had cut out the cancer.

Chapter 8

Burton's Ghost Sits on Abigail's Shoulder

As much as Abigail hated getting up early and preparing breakfast; getting the wood, stoking the stove, shooing the chickens off their nests to get the eggs, and setting the table in the summer kitchen, she was bound and determined to do it well so there would be no complaints.

She was carrying another person with her as she struggled to do the chores and live up to her promise of working hard. The baby slowed her down with every step she took. It was living off her, draining all her energy and a good part of her body's reserves. But she refused to let that divert her from her farm duties.

"Hi Abigail," William said as he sat at the table.

"Hello. I'm sorry I fell asleep on your shoulder in the barn last night." At the same time she placed a plate of fried eggs and bacon in front of him.

He smiled at her. "That's okay." The moment she set the plate down he cut the eggs with the side of his fork and sliced into the ham with his knife. "This looks so good."

Abigail leaned back on the sink, folded her arms over her chest and stared at William. "I hope you like your eggs that way," she said. "I turned them over easy so they would be cooked all the way through."

Then Noah came through the pantry and into the kitchen. He pulled the chair out with a great tug, until it remained motionless at his side. Then he picked it up and swung it towards the table as he sat hard on it when it came to a stop.

"I'm hungry girl. What da we got?" He sat at the table and whipped out his napkin and stuffed the end of it under his chin.

William stopped eating and paused to look at his boss before he started eating again. It was not so much that he wanted to be polite, as it was his reluctance to get in Noah's way at the breakfast table.

Abigail set the eggs and bacon in front of Noah. But the whites of the eggs were still raw and the slab of bacon was gristled with fat. She sensed that he was ignoring the short comings of her cooking because he was too hungry to argue about it. There would have been a time when she would have jumped to fix what was wrong, but now her power to care about what she did around the house faded away little by little.

After the breakfast was over the two men went out the door and into the fields to attend to the morning chores. Abigail was left to clean up and straighten up the kitchen.

As the days went on, it was getting harder and harder for her to do everything she had to do. Even though she did all her chores she did them with resentment. She found herself slamming the dishes down in the cabinet, scrubbing the clothes so hard that they tore, and pressing so hard on the windows that she broke through the glass. Her frustration grabbed a hold of her and made her look into the mirror of her heart. It was then that she realized what she was doing. She collapsed to the floor and started to cry.

Then, suddenly she got up off the floor and went to the pantry and looked into the corner of the little room, moved the broom out of the way and picked up the broken courting stick. She held it lovingly in her hands and started to weep again. After a while she sniffled and stopped crying. It brought back memories of Lawrence and the surprise and joy she felt when he gave it to her as a present. She picked it up and talked into it; "Lawrence, come back home. I need you."

She laughed at her strange behavior and took in a deep breath. Wouldn't it be wonderful if we could talk to the people we love somehow, by talking into a stick and they would hear us, she thought. These fanciful notions are coming to me because of the moonlight that I was exposed to last night. She smiled to herself and placed the stick back in the dark corner of the pantry.

Then she moved on to dust the windows. The sun was climbed into the September sky; it struggled to pull itself into a low arc even though it was past noon. The winter season was close on its heels, threatening it with a snowy white drape of sleep.

The oaks and elms shed their leaves as she stood in the window, and she knew from those signs that her time was growing short. She was a long distance runner, having anxiety, now that she was getting a glimpse of the finish line.

A tap on the window just below her waist startled her and she jumped back into the rocking chair. It skidded across the floor and slammed into the fireplace. She snapped the dust rag in the air and put it in her apron for safe keeping, then with great care tip-toed back to the window.

A man in a beaver top hat and mutton chop sideburns, stood at the window staring into the living room. He had his thumbs hooked to the inside of his vest which made his silver sheriff's badge bulge out and reflect the sunlight.

Abigail bent towards the window and shouted loud enough so he could hear her. "Can I help you sir?"

"Yes ma'am. I'd like to ask you a couple of questions. If you don't mind."

"All right. Come around to the front door. The summer kitchen is being closed down for the winter."

He passed the window and sauntered around to the front of the house. The door was a six panel arched door weighing over two-hundred pounds. And Abigail slowly opened it and then stared at the sheriff. She stood in the entrance and leaned on the massive wooden piece. "Yes," she said as she slid into the opening between the entrance and the sill of the door.

"I'd like to come in and talk to you about something." He reached up and grabbed hold of the inside of the door to steady himself.

"If you insist." Abigail swung the heavy door open and let him in, and then she slammed it shut.

"Well, let me get to the point." He switched from one foot to the other as he talked and then reached into his vest pocket and dangled the locket in front of her. "We found this silver heart shaped locket in the pocket of a man that was in the Packardville Road cemetery. The locket was silver with Abigail's June moonstone set in the middle of it. Etched on the cover was a dragonfly.

After asking around the village the constable had come to the conclusion that the locket belonged to Abigail. He was determined to uncover the truth of the mysterious jewelry no matter who he offended.

"It has your name engraved on the inside. I was wondering if you knew anything about it. We're relocating the graves and came across it when it fell out of the man's pocket as we attempted to put him in a casket."

Abigail picked the necklace from his hand and unfastened it. "Yes, this is mine."

"Then can you tell me how he got it?" With that he sat down on the rocker and stared smugly at her.

"I… I…don't know." All she could do was to look at the keepsake dangling off of the gold chain. To her it was just as much of a mystery as it was to the sheriff because she didn't know what Noah had done.

"Did you know him?"

"No." She walked over to the detective and dropped the locket into his open palm.

"Then how did he get it?" He looked straight into her shifty eyes.

Then she turned her back to the sheriff as she recalled past happenings. "I was married recently and there were people from all over at my wedding. Maybe he stole it then, or there was a time when my husband fed all these strangers that came up the road, maybe it was one of them, or—"

"That's all right Miss. Can I talk to your husband?" He got up from the chair and it continued to rock.

"He's not here anymore. He left."

"It's going to be kind of difficult to talk to him if he's not around." He walked to the front door and just before he left he turned and faced Abigail. "Don't leave the county. Make yourself available. I might want to talk to you again."

"Yes sir." As he was about to leave a sinking feeling came over her.

He stopped at the entrance to light his pipe and look at her through the smoke. "A lot of bodies were swept down the river."

After the sheriff had left she collapsed in the rocking chair and stared into the ashes of the fireplace. My mother and father might have been swept away in that flood. Even in death I can't hold onto anybody. Everybody gets swept away from me never to return.

In spite of that, she looked down at her belly and smiled. She imagined the baby all safe and secure in her womb, asleep, sucking its thumb, cuddled up to the wall of her tummy. She knew immediately that she would defend and protect this unborn thing that squirmed deep in her gut, as the heart beat, feet kicked, and forehead nudged its little sea cocoon. She had become a lioness, and would do anything to survive and attack anybody that threatened that existence.

The officer's visit pushed her to sit down and write the letter to the school that Daniel had mentioned. She picked up the straight pen with the split nib and dipped it into the India ink from the small glass ink well. Occasionally she would blot the pen with the blotter. She began to scratch out her message;

New Athens, Connecticut
November 19, 1865

Dear Mr. Fitch
Fitch's Home for Soldier's
And Orphans
Darien, Connecticut

Sir, —I always wished that I was a child again just working in the fields, sorting the vegetables, watching the plants grow, and especially teaching Lawrence, my step brother, to read from the McGuffey Reader. And that specifically is why I am writing this letter. For all his life I taught him about the morals of the stories in the Reader, and I believe that he became a better man because of it. His love of reading and learning did him well when he went into the Army. I also taught drawing, dancing, singing, sewing and philosophy in our local church on Sunday. The pastor, Reverend Albert Finney, I'm sure will give me a good reference if you require it.

I'm sure, Mr. Fitch, the students will love me, as much as I will love them. The poem 'Mary's Lamb' comes to mind from the First Reader. I can be firm but also kind to my students, just like Mary was to her lamb.

And just like Mr. Post that found Mary as a baby and cared and raised her and taught her to read the Bible, I likewise will care, raise, and educate my pupils. Some day they will do the same for other disadvantaged children, so the tradition of learning and caring can be passed on to the next generation.

Kindness is the theme of the McGuffey Reader. The care of the children of our fallen soldiers should be all important, as I know it is in your school.

I will get to the point at hand, if you don't mind the short letter. The fact of the matter is that I would like you to consider hiring me as a teacher at you school, because of my familiarity with the McGuffey Reader, which I know you use extensively, and my experience with the teaching arts.

Any references' that you might need can be gotten easily and passed on to

you.

Sincerely, Abigail Armstrong

Chapter 9

Snowwoman Born

The letter was burning in her hand and she had to mail it before she burst. She ran out the front door and went to the back of the house and past the summer kitchen. She headed for the barn to harness the horse and head into town. As she walked through the barn door she saw Daniel spearing hay with a pitch fork.

"Daniel would you take me into town?"

"Sure Miss Abby. As soon as I hitch the horse to the wagon." He threw the pitch fork into a bale of hay and then went over and lifted the harness off of the stall. It jingled and the leather harness squeaked at the same time as he positioned it over the head and on the chest of the horse. The reins snapped when he threw them at the seat. Everything was ready and they got up onto the bench.

Without delay she grabbed the reins. They felt slippery and hard to handle. "Well here we go," she said as she snapped the reins over the horse's rump. She imagined the horse as Pegasus, with large wings pulling the carriage along into the sky and plopping down all of a sudden in the center of town.

"Miss Abby wouldn't you rather have me drive?" He asked. "You got enough doin' with that baby in your belly."

Abigail pulled up on the reins, and leashed the wagon to the side of the road.

She turned to Daniel and handed him the reins. "I think you're right. I do need some takin' care of." It was hard for her to admit her short comings. Maybe Daniel could get us there faster, she thought

"I'll go slow Miss Abby."

"Okay. Not too slow. I want to get to the mailman as soon as we can."

They pulled into town next to the Post Office.

The shop was a simple one story wood building with a window on each side looking like big wide eyes and a roof that leaned down and over the porch seeming to imitate the brim of a postman's hat. On top of the porch was a sign; Post Office and Store.

To Abigail the store reminded her of a giant's round visor-type hat that the postmen wore on their rounds as they delivered the mail. Daniel sat on the buckboard in anticipation of her return.

Next to the door as Abigail entered was a plaque that read; Building, Charles King Merchant Built 1865. The smell of cinnamon, sweet marjoram, summer savory, chopped onions and parsley coming from the tall glass containers and filled the store with sweet and sour aromas. The sight of fruits and vegetables' sliced thin and threaded on strings caught her eye. They were white and red and pink.

She walked over to a glass container that had cloves in it and lifted the top off. The sweet pungent smell filled her nostrils which made her smile. Then she lifted off the glass top from another decanter and the biting fresh taste of mint engulfed her face as she closed her eyes taking pleasure in the exotic aroma.

"Hi Charlie," Abigail said as she walked up to the post office section of the building. Charlie was on the other side of the cage. He was around twenty-five and had a simple starched white shirt on with an ascot tie hanging off his neck, and a storekeeper's apron on over that. His hair was parted in the middle, and what set him apart from every other young man of the time, was his clean shaven, almost medicinal appearance.

"Hay Abigail. I heard the good news. How are you feeling?"

"Okay. I just feel bloated like a fat cow."

"That will pass, you'll see," he said. "What can I do for you?"

How could he know, she thought. He's not a doctor, just a postman. She looked down at the waist high counter, afraid that he would see the scorn in her eyes. "I want to mail this letter to Darien Connecticut. How much would it cost?"

"Let's see." He took the letter out of her hand through the wire cage and slid it on a scale. "That will be three cents."

She pulled open her silk reticule handbag, and then reached in, moving around her handkerchief, fan and perfume bottle while she looked for some money. A flush crept over her face and she began to sweat. "I could have sworn I had some money in here," she said. "Sorry Charlie. I don't have any change."

"That's okay Abigail. You can owe me." He turned around and called his dog. "Puck come over here."

All of a sudden a white fox terrier with a black snout and ears jumped up on the stool next to Charlie. He had a little jacket-like bag strapped around his body and it had pockets on each side. Charlie slipped the letter into one of the pockets.

Abigail smiled at the dog as it wagged its tail and then scratched its belly with its hind foot. "Is he going to deliver my mail?"

"Oh no. It's just a way that Puck can feel useful." He said. "I let him carry some of the mail before I transfer it onto the train."

"Can I come around and pet him?"

"Sure."

Charlie opened up the cage door and let her in. She walked with care as she brushed by the large canvas bags marked, No. 2 U.S Mail. The walls were filled with wooden bins; eight slots across and eight slots down. Every hole was filled with mail or a rolled up package. Abigail brushed by a stack of packages and her dress snagged on them and pulled them off onto the floor. "I'm sorry Charlie," she said "I didn't see them there."

"That's okay Abby. No harm done." He bent over and gathered them up in his arms as if they were an infant and then bent over at the waist as he let them go on the table next to the sitting stools.

Abigail bent over and started to pet Puck. He was all curled up on top of one of the canvass mail bags. His thin white tail wagged energetically and he looked up at her with big brown eyes as he moaned "ar-owl-wow-wow!" Then he got up and sniffed her pregnant belly.

"Puck, Stop that!" Charlie shouted.

"It's okay Charlie. He's just curious."

Suddenly the bell that was attached on the door rang as a customer stomped over the wooden floor headed right for the Post Office. It was Noah.

Abigail all at once scooted under the counter just below Charlie. Her head was in her chest and she could feel pressure on her pregnant belly. She looked up at him and pulled at his pant leg. "Make believe that you haven't seen me. Please Charlie."

Charlie looked down at her and half nodded and then whispered. "Okay. Don't worry."

"Hey Charlie," Noah said. "Have you seen Abigail? The wagon is outside and Daniel is sitting in it. Said she came in here."

"Maybe she was looking at something in the store and decided not to buy anything and then left," Charlie said, while he rummaged around with the mail and looked at it as he spoke.

"Daniel said that she was going to mail a letter. Do you know anything about that?" By now Noah leaned close into the cage and Abigail saw above her, the sleeve of his shirt through a crack in the wood.

"She…ah." Abigail looked up at Charlie and nodded that it was okay to tell about the letter. "Oh, I forgot, she didn't have enough money for it so I said she could owe me."

"Let me see it," Noah said as he leaned closer against the cage.

"Puck come over here." The dog trotted over to Charlie happy to be doing its job. It looked up at him and wagged its tail so hard that its hind legs scraped along the wooden floor. After that Puck licked Abigail's face, welcoming her to his under the counter world, of letters and burlap bags.

Charlie reached into the left pocket of the pouch and came up with the mail. He held it in his thumb and forefinger.

Noah reached through the cage and snatched the letter from his fingers. "I'll pay for the postage," Noah said, and at the same time read the address on the front. "How much?"

"Three cents."

"There you go." Noah handed him the change and then put the letter in his pocket.

"Don't you want to send it," Charlie shouted as Noah turned and headed for the door.

"No," he said just before he slammed the door, making the bell ring frantically as he left.

Abigail got out from under the counter and looked out the small side window. Noah got on the seat of the wagon, reached into his pocket and pulled out the letter and tore it in five pieces and then threw it in the street.

A small desperate voice came from deep inside of her. It was a voice that she had never heard before, a voice that seemed as if it came from the deepest part of her soul. "Oh no. What did he do?" After that she leaned her cheek on the window and began to sob.

Charlie walked over to her and rested his hand on her shoulder. "What's the matter Abigail?"

She turned and looked up at him. "He just destroyed my future and threw it in the street. That letter was important to me and now it's just a memory."

Charlie pulled her close to his chest. "Don't worry we'll fix it." He said. "Here, sit down at the desk and write the letter again, we'll send it out with the next mail train."

Charlie set up Abigail with his favorite quill pen and paper and a desk to write her letter. The moment she sat down she began writing the letter the same exact way that she originally had written it. The scratch of the pen on the paper filled the room. When she was done she handed it to Charlie with a big grin on her face. "There you go Charlie. Thanks, I don't know how I can pay you back."

"It was my pleasure. I'm a firm believer that we should help each other. After all we all breathe the same air and we are all children looking for a way to happiness. And besides that slavery was abolished in Connecticut in 1848, right?"

She turned to face him. "That's really profound Charlie."

"Oh I guess I sort of got influenced by this writer I've been reading lately, Henry David Thoreau. In his book "Walden," he says 'I had three chairs in my house; one for solitude, two for friendship, three for society.' I let you sit in the chair I reserved for friendship, because I could see that you needed a friend."

"Thanks for that. I sure needed somebody's help," she said. "I better get going; I've got a long way to walk to get back to the farm."

"I won't hear of it. I'll take you back home after we deliver the mail to the train."

"Thanks."

The old clock at the back of the room chimed three times. Abigail assumed that at 3 o'clock it was time for Charlie to deliver some of his mail but her assumption was wrong because when he lifted the mail bags they were only half full. It was then that she realized that Charlie was doing her a special favor.

"Come on Puck there's some mail we have to deliver." Puck put his paws on Charlie's leg and stretched and yawned waiting for his letters to be dropped in his little satchel. When that was done he smiled and walked to the door and waited for Charlie.

"We're already Abigail," Charlie said. He had hold of two canvas bags slung over his back when he approached the door. He looked like a small camel. "Abigail, open the door so I can get through?"

"Sure Charlie." She pushed open the door making the bell ring while Puck ran outside and jumped on the seat of the mail wagon. One jump and he was on the seat. He seemed so proud of himself with his chest all puffed out.

As Puck sat there looking at the post office he thought, 'Charlie better hurry up or else we're going to be late. But it seems strange to be delivering mail so late in the afternoon.' His eyes stared intently at the dawdling humans pushing through the door.

The postal wagon was a closed in box-type of carriage with the door in the center and a small glass window on each side of the door. It had big letters on the side, Postal Wagon. And bigger letters on the door, U.S. Mail. On one side of the coach it had the letters; R.F.D #1. Around the top trim of the wagon was painted the patriotic colors of red white and blue, and on each side of the door was a red white and blue Eagle.

The two large draft horses stamped their back hoofs and swished their tails against the last living cold weather flies. Their big round eyes bulged and their hearts beat fast in anticipation of pulling the mail through the countryside. They fidgeted and pawed the mud. This job brought excitement into their animal lives.

Charlie opened the door to the carriage and threw in the two sacks of mail. They skidded across the floor and banged into the door on the other side. "Abigail, get inside and sit down quietly while I make a few stops," he said. "We're not supposed to take anybody with us that's not a postal employee but if you just stay quiet and out of sight I guess it'll be alright."

Abigail put her foot on the step, swung open the door and went in and sat down on one of the burlap bags. Then she turned, and talked through the closed window. Her question hung in the air. "Will you get in trouble for this Charlie?" He looked like a phantom through the ice frosted window.

His voice got louder. "I have to do this for you. It's the right thing to do." Then he got into the seat of the carriage, and after that Abigail could feel the lurch of the wagon as it was pulled down the road by the big horses, and she imagined the horse's muscles rippling. She heard the sound of their mouth's chomp and click on the steel bit and hoofs clop on the icy road.

I won't let Noah rein me like those horses. This is my body and I'll make my own decisions and become a teacher. What I've seen he'll never see. He's just a farmer and that's all he'll ever be, she thought.

Lounging among the newspapers, letters and periodicals, deep in the bowls of the carriage, she became a child protected from the outside world. She was physically protected from the cold by the insulating effects of the papers all around her, but more than that she became a womb within a womb as she stretched her arms over her head and let out a deep sigh of satisfaction.

She picked a letter from the pile of mail and looked at the address and the name Barbra Kendall. It smelled of lilac perfume and was a store bought envelope. The name pricked at her brain. Then, in an instant she remembered, she had seen that same name in the cemetery when they were trying to find her parents. This must be a letter having something to do with one of their relatives.

The sound of sliding piles of paper and the musty smell of envelopes was the last thing she remembered before she dove into the lives of the people that had scribbled on the envelopes in front of her.

The ability to pick up a letter and see the name and imagine who they were and what they did became intoxicating; Dozier, a family that has something to do with gold or silver, Gibson, maybe having to do with guns, Herring, could be a family that were fishermen? Spencer, seems like a name that belongs to a doctor, Vickery, a name given to a priest or a place where a priest lives, Wells, something to do with water or farms, Wise, of course people who are wise or teachers knowledgeable about the world, Woodward, people who make their living from the woods.

She laughed at her imagination. Maybe some of those people are who I think they are, she thought.

All of a sudden the wagon stopped. Charlie opened the door. "Smells like snow doesn't it?" He asked as he pulled a bag of mail from the pile that was in front of her "I've got to get you home." Before she could answer he had slammed the door shut and was gone.

Just before she got into the Postal Wagon she noticed the sky being gray and heavy with snow. Now, when she looked outside she saw the white puffy flakes fall by the windows of the wagon. They were big and round and pregnant with moisture. And they clung to the wheels of the carriage and cradled themselves around the limbs of the naked trees.

Charlie opened a door to the general store and dropped the bag inside. Abigail cracked the carriage door a little and hollered through it. "Charlie if you want, I can stay at the Post Office until the storm blows over."

"No, no, it's okay. I have to get you home. It'll be alright." He ran back to the wagon and Abigail could feel the carriage tip to one side and hear the springs squeak as he jumped up onto the seat. She heard the snap of the reins and the jingle of the harnesses on the horses while they turned in the road, heading back to the farm. Again he stopped the coach. She could hear the crunch of the snow as he jumped off the seat. "Here, cuddle with Puck. I'm afraid I'll lose him in all this snow." He handed the dog to her through the door.

Puck whimpered in her arms just before he jumped off and plopped himself down into a pile of burlap mail sacks, but not before he had turned around a few times to settle into the most comfortable place in the center of the bags. Then he gave out a long satisfied sigh. At the end of all this jockeying around, for a comfy spot, he looked up at her with his sad eyes and then wagged his little rat tail.

Charlie made a side trip to the train station before bringing Abigail back to the farm. Abigail could hear the whoosh of the steam coming from the steam engine and the squeal of steel wheels on the tracks and the clang of the bell on the front of the locomotive. The industrial smell of oil and coal covered the Postal Wagon.

He reached in and pulled out the last two mail bags. Just as he did, Abigail managed to scrunch up against the inside of the wagon so the Post Master wouldn't see her. Charlie pulled away from the station and then stopped on the side of the road, got down and opened the door to the Postal Carriage. "Well we're all done. Now I can get you home."

"Thanks Charlie."

"The snow warden is packin' down the snow on the roads so we shouldn't have any trouble getting you home."

Abigail pulled down the glass window in the door and looked at the road in front of them. A uniformed man sat in a carriage, with what looked like, a gigantic rolling pin being towed by the wagon.

It reminded her of one of the wooden rolling pins that she used in the kitchen to make pies with. It clattered along as it compressed the snow on the road, making a smooth sound, like when you run your hand over a bolt of silk cloth.

The Postal carriage leaned to one side and then to the other as its wagon wheels dug into the wet snow. It coated the wheels with a white tire of frozen ice. She could hear the snap of the whip while Charlie hollered; "Pull gentleman. Pull." It cut through the road at a slow steady pace until they reached the farm.

"Thanks Charlie. I'll never forget your kindness," Abigail said as she closed the door to the carriage. The wagon pulled away while Abigail went into the front door of the house.

William was sitting on the rocker in the living room, in front of the fire. "Hi Bill. What are you doing here?"

"I'm waiting for Noah." He smiled at her and stabbed the logs with the poker.

"Hey, I've got an idea. Let's build a snowman."

"I don't think I've ever done that before. Besides I don't think Noah will like us wasting our time building a snowman when we should be doing our chores." He stood up and Abigail grabbed his hand and pulled him out onto the porch.

"Don't worry about Noah. He's an old fuddy-duddy. Point you face into the sky and let the snowflakes tickle your nose. Go ahead do it. Nobody will see you," she said, noticing that he seemed embarrassed.

"They're wet and big. I bet they'll make a great snowman." He ran off the porch and started to roll up the snow into a ball.

Abigail followed his lead and then they were both in the snow creating a man. The cold stung her nose and the snow froze her hands.

They put a large ball on the bottom, a little smaller snowball in the middle and a snowball the size of a human head on top.

"He doesn't look like anything," Abigail said. She tipped her head from side to side.

"I'll fix that," he said. He trudged through the snow and went into the barn. By this time, ten minutes had gone by and the snow had stopped. He had an armful of things that he dropped in the snow in front of their handiwork.

"We'll slick him up so he looks like something." Abigail bent down and picked up the chimney top hat that William had given her and pieces of coal. She made coal eyes, a nose and a coal smile and then stuck the top hat on his head.

"Wait, wait, I've got an idea. Turn around. I'll tell you when you can turn back to see my idea.

"Okay." She turned around and covered her eyes with the palms of her hands.

Mean while William sliced a red pepper in half, put the halves on the chest and packed in the eggplant so that the snowman looked like a pregnant snow women with the black eggplant sticking out from its belly. She could hear the packing of the snow and the crunch and crackle of the peppers being sliced. And she wondered what those strange sounds meant.

"All right turn around. What do you think? It's you."

Abigail began to laugh. "Oh Bill you're so bad." She bent down and made a snow ball and then threw it in his face.

He gasped. "That's cold."

"Is that how I look?" She rested her hands on her stomach and stared at the snow woman.

"Oh no, not really. I thought you'd think it was funny." He looked back at his handiwork.

"I love that you had the imagination to make a snow woman." She stood still, not saying a word.

"Are you all right Abigail? You seem sad." He kicked the snow in front of him to make a path to her.

She circled the snow woman, and as she did she looked down and then stopped and let out a deep sigh. "Do you know what your parents look like?" she asked. "I never saw my parents. I was adopted when I was a baby."

"Yes I knew them. They were a strange combination. My mother Mary was a little lady with sky blue eyes and dark black hair. My father, Edward, was a tall man with a large handlebar mustache and steely grey eyes that never smiled."

"Even though they seemed strange to you, you at least saw them."

"Yep." Bill walked over to the snow woman and changed the position of the top hat so it sat more on the top of its head.

"What's wrong with me that they wanted to get rid of me?" Tears ran down her cheeks and she sniffled a few times.

"Nothing is wrong with you. Things just happen and we don't have any control over them, that's all." William wrapped his arms around her and put her head on his chest. "There's always a reason for what happens even though we can't see it now, it will reveal itself to us later on."

Chapter 10

Her Little Letter Calls to Her

The next morning Abigail woke up early so that she could look out the window to see their snow woman, and to recall the fun and excitement they had making something that was their creation separate from the workings of the farm.

But her stomach dropped and a sinking feeling grabbed a hold of her when she looked out the window and saw the remains of the little snow creature spread over the ground. The hat was next to the barn, the eggplant was sliced in half, and the peppers were next to the porch along with the pieces of coal. It no longer had any life to it. Its organs were strewn all over the farm. To her it was like seeing a real human hacked to pieces.

She knew, or suspected, that it was Noah who broke up their little white creation. She imagined him being startled by the snow woman and taking a shovel to it, splitting it in half in a fit of rage. And then scooping up the black eyes and mouth in the shovel and throwing them in the snow.

She shook her head and became sad as if the snow woman was a relative that had passed away. The destruction of the snow woman was a metaphor for what was going on at the farm.

The morning at once warmed, melting the snow on the roof so it dribbled off of the eves and thawed out the ground so that the grass underneath came back green. The New England weather was living up to its changeable reputation.

A week or so had gone by and all that time Abigail imagined the image of the letter in the mail bag like a little flat person with its tiny eyes darting around waiting to be picked up and carried to its destination, and then at last opening up its belly and flinging its precious words at Mr. Fitch's eyes, and Mr. Fitch being so in love with her message that he at once, sat down and wrote back a letter inviting her to his school.

Now that the first snow had fallen, Abigail was gripped with a frantic, nervous feeling in her gut surrounding the baby, which pulled her thoughts in the direction of the Fitch school. After all, she thought, that was the bargain that she had with Noah, which was that when the first snow fell, she would be off. Something told her that the reply to the letter was there at the Post Office.

She harnessed the horse to the carriage, as best as she could, with her belly from time to time getting in the way.

When she at last got onto the road, the mud smelled damp and stagnant and seemed to be a threatening black-brown color. It protested being trudged over by clinging onto the horse's hoofs and wagon wheels and belching from its stomach with slow sucking sounds. To her it seemed alive and doing Noah's bidding since it was trying to keep her from leaving the farm because its black fingers reached up from the underground and tried to pull everything to a standstill.

She whipped Rebel. He pulled the wagon as hard as he could. The muscles in his legs tightened like rubber bands, while the power from his back pulled the carriage behind him like it was nothing more than a little toy. His eyes got bigger and white foamy sweat squeezed out from under the leather harness.

He was determined to please Abigail, given that it was the only thing he knew how to do well. He picked up speed in spite of the muddy road.

Abigail could feel the excitement while she held tight to the reins. In her mind's eye she could see the letter sitting on the counter in the Post Office. It was shaking and popping off the counter in anticipation of being read. Like a little puppy, it turned its belly up to the ceiling and waited to be petted. She knew that it would lick her hand as soon as she opened the flaps on its tummy and read the words.

Mean while, Rebel, only doing his job, took the curve too sharp and fast. The carriage tipped over on its side and skidded to a stop in the mud on the edge of the road. Abigail's world tipped sideways and then just as sudden went dark. She lay there in the mud next to the broken bones of the carriage. The wheels were splintered and the seat broke in half. She could hear moaning and then realized that it was her.

"The baby… the baby is she all right?" In her confusion she kept asking herself the same question over and over again, as if somebody from inside her head would answer the question.

A hand from the world of the living reached into her world and splashed water on her face. "Abigail are you all right?" William asked. "The baby is okay. You just got a bump on your head."

"Oh Lawrence you came home. I missed you so much." She reached up and grabbed William and kissed him passionately and then realizing that it was

William. She stopped and pulled away. "Where am I?" She blinked her eyes and looked around.

"You had an accident. The carriage tipped over. But you're all right." With that, he picked her up and put her on the horse that he had ridden in on.

"Poor Rebel he's hurt," she said.

A high pitched scream came from the horse's throat. It thrashed around trying to get up, stretched its neck and jingled its harness while it slid in the slippery mud.

"I've got to put that suffering horse out of his misery." William walked over to Rebel and pointed his revolver at its head. He shot the horse and then stood over it as the pistol dangled by his side. "I hate to kill anything but I had to do that."

"Yes I know." Abigail recognized the Navy Colt pistol as the same kind that she shot Burton with. The incident triggered memories of a marriage, a killing, a trip, and the loss of her husband. To her it was more than just a horse with a broken leg being put away; it was the passing away of a happy time in her life. After all, Rebel had pulled the wagon that brought Lawrence back to the farm. The winged Pegasus had been killed.

"Do you want me to bring you back home Abigail?"

"No, I want to get my letter. Please bring me to the Post Office."

"Okay if you insist. Are you sure you're all right?"

"Yes."

"Hold on. How do you know that the letter is there?"

"I just know, that's all."

He walked in front of his horse and led him by the reins while Abigail sat in the saddle and looked out at the horizon like a lookout in the crow's nest of a ship.

The road straightened out after that. It got flatter and wider the closer they got to town.

Then it dawned on her what had just happened. "I'm sorry about that kiss. I thought you were somebody else."

"That's okay Abigail, I enjoyed it." William smiled.

Abigail could feel her face flush and the warmth of embarrassment form around her neck. After that the only sound that could be heard was the clop of the horse's hoofs and his occasional snort.

"We're here. Let me down."

William helped her slide off the horse and onto the ground. "Do you want me to come in the office with you?"

"No, I'll be all right." She stepped on the porch and then pushed open the door, and as soon as she went inside she confronted Charlie; "My letter, I know it's here," she shouted.

Charlie jumped back, being startled by her question. He had been sorting mail behind the cage. "Oh…Abigail it's you."

"My letter. I saw it in a day dream. It was here in a mail bag waiting for me to pick it up."

"Hold on a minute I'll check." He walked to the back of the station where a mail bag had been dropped off earlier that morning. His heavy hob nail boots thumped across the wooden floor. The swish of the bag being dragged across the floor drew Abigail's attention to Charlie as he opened the top of the leather bag and dumped out the mail in front of her.

"Is that it?" She pointed her finger at a letter on the top of the pile. "Ooh, that looks like it." By now she had bent over the pile, and had kneeled down in the mountain mail.

"I don't see it Abigail," Charlie said.

She straightened up and stared in Charlie's face. She wanted to say that he was incompetent and that the letter was there somewhere. She stopped herself from doing that because she remembered the kindness that he had done, so she swallowed her disappointment. Maybe he was right and the vision she saw was just wishful thinking.

"Thanks Charlie." She left quick, not even looking back before she swung open the door and went out on the porch. The bell on the door kept ringing and she wanted to reach up and tear it off of its spring. Tears of frustration streamed down her face as she stood on the deck.

"Come on William let's go back to the farm." He hunched his shoulders and lowered his head. Abigail's disappointment floated towards him like a dark cloud.

Charlie's voice without warning lifted the building into the air, or that's the way it sounded to Abigail. "I found it Abigail. I found it." He banged through the door with the letter in his hand. "It was in the special delivery slot and I forgot about it."

When he put it in her hand it was like he had handed her a fist full of diamonds. Her hands shook as she opened up the letter. At this point she was more nervous than ever because she all of a sudden thought, what if he said no.

She tore open the letter and as she kept reading the tears poured out even more.

"I'm sorry Abigail. Is it bad news?" Charlie put his hand on her shoulder at the same time that William walked up the steps. "I think she got bad news." Charlie said.

Abigail sat hard on the steps and sobbed into the palms of her hands with the letter being soaked by her tears.

"What can I do to help you Abigail?" William asked.

"You can help me pack. Its yes. He said as soon as I can he'd like to see me at the school." Abigail jumped up and hugged Charlie, hugged William, and then went over and kissed the horse on the nose.

Chapter 11

Men Help Her

It was a man's world, and improbable as it might seem, men were the people that were helping her reach her goal of becoming a teacher. None of the women that she knew from school or from church dared to lend a hand. Whether they were embarrassed or afraid of the consequences of aligning themselves with her, Abigail did not know.

She marveled at Charlie and William's resolve to help. They had people that they had to answer to but they chose to ignore the consequences. She wondered if one or both of them had a crush on her. Maybe that was the reason for their attentiveness.

"Abigail, I want you to ride in the Postal wagon so I can bring you home," Charlie said. "I'll be right back." He ran to the back of the building and she could hear him jingle the harnesses and slap the leather against the horses while he got the wagon ready.

"I better give him a hand," William said. Then he left with his horse being pulled behind him as he disappeared around the back of the building.

Five minutes later the Postal Wagon rattled up to the front of the Post Office with the two men riding on the seats and William's horse tethered to the back of the wagon. Charlie looked down and said; "Your carriage awaits Madame." They both laughed.

William jumped down off the elevated seat and held the door of the carriage open, acting like a coachman. He bowed to her as she stepped into wagon. "I hope the accommodations are satisfactory Ma'am."

"Yes, they seem quite satisfactory dear sir." She stuck her nose into the air pretending to be snooty royalty. Then she settled in the carriage among the letters and papers. They crackled and rustled under her back. "You may precede good man." She held her hand in the air with her pinky raised.

"Yes, very good." He shut the door and climbed back up on the seat.

They headed out of town and Abigail could see bundles of mail being tossed off of the wagon and landing on the door steps of some of the buildings as they passed by.

It wasn't long until they reached the farm. Abigail could not control her joy. She kept smiling and could not stop. Her heart beat fast in anticipation of the new adventure that she would be having at the Fitch School for Orphans.

William opened the door and held her hand as he guided her small foot onto the tiny step on the carriage and then onto the ground. "I'm so happy William." She wrapped her arms around his waist and then rested her head on his shoulder.

"I'm glad. You deserve some happiness. I think that school is just the place for you." His breath tickled her ear as he whispered into it.

When she backed away she could see that his face was flushed with embarrassment. "Oh, I'm sorry. I didn't mean to make you feel uncomfortable."

"It's all right Abigail. I understand." He turned and went to the back of the carriage and unhitched his horse and proceeded to bring it back to the barn.

"Thanks Charlie," she shouted, waving a good bye, as she ran through the front door and then up the stairs and into her room.

She pulled the luggage off of the top shelf of the closet and plopped them on the bed. There was a round hat box, a Gladstone bag, a cream colored suitcase and a red and blue patterned carpet bag. These were the only suitcases that she thought she would need. After all she came to the farm when she was a child with just the baby blanket wrapped around her.

She opened the leather, cotton lined suitcase and laid all the neatly folded clothes in the bottom of it and when she was finished she fastened the crocodile straps tightly into their buckles between all the rivets and studs on the luggage. While she folded some clothes and placed them into the suitcase, she just threw others into the carpet bag.

On the floor of the closet was a hat that she loved and was not willing to leave behind because it was the hat that she wore when she and Lawrence went to New York. It was a white bonnet with a pink rose attached to the side and it fastened to your head by a long pink ribbon. She stripped off the tissue paper that was protecting the precious hat and gingerly put it in the round hat box. She smiled when she looked at it. It smells sweet and flowery, she thought.

Her feet, only by a hair's breath, touched the floor; she was so enchanted by the thought of her new adventure, and so excited and happy that she began to laugh and cry at the same time. While she stuffed her clothes into the carpet bag she heard the heavy footsteps of two people coming up the stairs. She turned, and her mood changed. She sensed trouble in the sound of the deliberate gait of the weighty boots.

Noah stood in the doorway with Daniel just behind him. "Abigail, I understand you are going to leave the farm." He had his thumbs hooked to the straps on his overall jeans.

"Yes." She closed the carpet bag with a sudden snap. "Benjamin Fitch wrote me back and said that he wanted me to come and teach at his school."

"Does he know you're pregnant?" With that, he took another step closer to Abigail. His words were just another arrow that pierced her heart and gave her pause.

She thought about it and sat hard on the feather mattress. "It never occurred to me that it would matter," she said. She felt him close off the room, which made it harder to breathe, harder to defend herself. Then she looked up at him in defiance. After that she snatched a pillow from the head of the bed and cradled it against her chest and looked down at the floor.

"Besides, you don't have any money. How do you expect to get there?" He exchanged a knowing look and a smirk when he looked back at Daniel. Daniel had learned from being a slave at an early age that you never take sides. You just stare ahead and accept the situation.

Abigail had been pulled back to reality again. Her opportunity for freedom was snatched away by Noah. She sat staring at the rug while tears welled up in her eyes. After Noah had done his damage he left, but Daniel stayed, standing in the shadow of the half closed door.

"Don't cry missy. I'll help you," he said.

"Daniel, you startled me. I didn't expect to see you behind the door." She threw the pillow back on the bed and stood up.

"I has some money I can give you. It's in my Posthole Bank." He ran out of the room and the next thing Abigail knew she saw him with a shovel digging up a fence post that was under the elm tree. He reached down into the hole and came up with a mason jar; all at once he stuck it under his arm.

She heard him clop up the stairs and then appear in her doorway.

"Here," he said. He held the jar out at arm's length.

"What is this Daniel?" Abigail took the glass jar and recognized the gold dollars with the feathered Indian head on one side and the # 1 on the opposite side. But mixed in between them were Pistareen Spanish silver coins that were hardly worth fifteen or twenty cents. They had crosses and crowns on their surfaces because they were from another time in the country's history.

"I thought these would help you." He hung his head trying not to look her straight in the eyes.

She knew that they would only help a little but she took them as if they were worth a great deal. These are everything he owns of any value, she thought.

"Thank you Daniel, these will help." She smiled as she placed them in the carpet bag.

"Is there anything else I can do for you Miss Abigail?"

"Yes." She rearranged her bags on the bed as she talked. "Would you bring me into town in the morning so I can catch the stage coach?"

"Yes ma'am. I'd be happy to."

When Abigail looked back up he was gone. After that she sat on the bed looking out the window and daydreaming about the Fitch school. Her luggage nudged her from the back as if to say that it was anxious to be on its way. Even the baby kicked in her belly trying to get her attention. But her thoughts were exploring the possibilities of the future, as uncertain as that might be.

The daydream was interrupted by the thump of boots coming up the stairs. Abigail thought that it was Daniel but when she turned around to face the door she saw William.

"Oh, William it's you." She got up and leaned on the bed post.

"I have something for you." He reached out and pushed a wad of bills into the palm of her hand.

"Oh, thank you William. I'll never be able to repay you." She began to unravel the money and count it. "There's over a hundred dollars in here." She smiled at him and then frowned.

"Yes I know," he said. "But it's not from me. It's from Noah."

"From Noah?" Without hesitation she threw the money on the bed as if it was contaminated.

"He gave it to me to give to you because I think he was ashamed of the way he has been treating you lately."

"I don't care. I don't want it."

William bent over the feather bed and plucked up the paper money. It made a crunching sound as he gathered it up. Then he walked over to Abigail and stuffed it back in her hand. "Here, make believe it's from me."

"Okay. But it still feels slimy."

"Just forget about Noah. Think of it as a gift from heaven sent to you coming from an unusual direction," he said with a smirk. "It's just paper but it can help you on your way to a new life no matter where it came from."

Abigail sat back on the bed again but this time William walked over to her and kissed her on the forehead. Afterward she whispered to herself as she watched him leave the room; "I'll miss him and Daniel."

She sat up the rest of the night and just stared out the window and dozed off once in a while. Until at last it was time to leave.

The yard had a new blanket of snow on it and a trail of foot prints led up to the farm house. They could only have been Daniel's boots that had made the path. On the edge of the morning skyline the bald forehead of the full moon was about to set in anticipation of the rising sun in the east.

"Morning Daniel," Abigail said as Daniel came into the room and lugged her bags down the stairs.

"Morning ma'am," he said over his shoulder. He struggled with the luggage, as it bumped down every step. He then dragged the bags out to the carriage.

Abigail walked with careful steps down the flight of stairs because her knees were knocking and her right hand trembled on the railing. Except for going to New York on her honeymoon, this was the only other time she had been away from home. She had gotten to the front door when a memory pulled her back into the living room.

"The Courting Stick," she whispered to herself. All at once she went back into the pantry and picked up the stick and nestled it under her arm as she made for the door. When she slammed the front door on her way out, a thick carpet of snow slid off the roof and plopped down at the bottom of the steps.

She crunched through the snow that was on the porch and swished the snow aside with her feet while she made a path to the carriage. She looked around for Noah but he was nowhere to be found. It was then that she realized, knowing him as well as she did, that he was too proud to see her off.

The new horse pulled the coach with enthusiasm, just as Rebel had done, but she was a mare and she pranced through the snow lifting her hooves high above the ground.

When finally they had reached the center of town and had pulled up in front of the Post Office they both sat motionless and stared straight ahead. "The stage coach should be here any minute now," Abigail said. She spoke into the air because she felt sadness on leaving Daniel behind and refused to let him see her tears.

"Yes ma'am."

At that moment the stage coach rumbled, jingled and broke the silence of the early morning as it pulled up in front of the Post Office. A large man in what seemed to be a beaver jacket a beaver top hat and heavy black boots said: "Everybody in the carriage if you please and all luggages on top so they can be tied and secured." It was a red wooden stage coach with bright colored yellow undercarriage and wheels. The inside bench seats could hardly hold four people comfortably let alone the three men and the two ladies that were going to occupy it.

Even as far away as the driver was from Abigail she could still smell the cloud of alcohol climbing down the stage coach with him. The springs squeaked and the coach groaned under the driver's weight while he climbed down to the ground. He turned and grabbed the grey leather sack of mail and threw it on the top of the coach. Another man on top tied all the bags and luggage that Daniel had thrown up to him securely on the black metal gate surrounding the cargo area.

Abigail got up into the coach with the help of Daniel. He held her arm steady while she stepped on the stair and then took her seat in the stage coach.

"Here you go ma'am," Daniel said as he handed her a lap blanket and then slid the foot warmer in along the floor. She smiled at him one last time as she got settled in her seat.

"Thank you Daniel."

"It's my pleasure ma'am," he said. "I'd wish you luck but I knows you don't need it. You're a woman now and you make your own luck." That was the last time she spoke to Daniel. He saw in her what she felt all along. She had the sense of being more in control, a feeling of looking down on a problem and not being as swayed by her emotions. She felt as if she were growing.

While she was pulling down the black leather curtain on the window the driver passed by, he stopped for a split second and swigged down a mouthful of whiskey. "Ah." He saw Abigail through the window and offered her a swig. He held the bottle in front of the open window. "Go head Miss, it'll do you good."

"No thanks." She rolled down the window. It seemed to keep some of the heat in the coach.

After that he climbed up into the boot of the stagecoach. The coach shook from side to side as if a tic had gotten on its back and it was trying to shake it off. Then the driver settled into the driver's seat with a loud thump and a deep sigh.

As a result the rest of the passengers got on and in the wagon. Two men sat on the top, in the cargo area, holding on tight, expecting a bumpy ride. Then an older lady got into the cab of the carriage. She sat opposite Abigail and removed her high feathered hat and put it on her lap. Next, three large men, one at a time, grabbed hold of the handholds and swung themselves into their seats.

Their boots scraped along the wooden floor as they settled into their places. Their personalities filled up the spots that they sat in; one man with muttonchops side burns leaned out the window and spit a mouthful of tobacco into the white virgin snow, making it turn a disgusting brown. Another man with a derby dress hat on and a well kept suit smoked his cigar until the smoke filled the cabin. A young boy, which sat on the floor, leaned up against the door. He had a slouch hat on, and was content to bury his head between his knees and fall asleep.

For some unexplained reason all the men had on loose gloves that seemed two or three sizes too large. Abigail thought that it was a way of keeping their hands away from the cold and she saw as the day went on, that she was right, because their gloves became so stiff from the bitter icy weather that the fingers of the gloves stuck straight out. When they tried to straighten them the gloves crackled.

She was warm in her quilted lap robe and her foot warmer but felt pushed against by the men that got on the stage coach. The coach began to move and she waved good bye to Daniel as it clattered down the main street.

A man with a red checkered coat on and a black sailor's hat leaned towards the man that was smoking the cigar, and said, "Hey, stow that cigar mate. We have two ladies aboard."

"But I'm not finished with it yet. You can see that can't you?"

He had a furrowed brow and a stare under that black hat that burned into the other man's eyes. "All I can see is that you're bothering the ladies," the sailor said.

In a flash he snuffed the end of the cigar against the wall of the stage coach. "Oh, I'm sorry I…" Then he cleared his throat and shuffled his feet. His face got red and he began to sweat. After the two men exchanged words, he stuffed the half smoked cigar into the small pocket of his vest.

Abigail and the other lady thanked the gentleman sailor and then settled down into their seats trying to cope with the bumpy ride. They leaned against the windows, and squirmed for a comfortable spot.

Chapter 12

Building a New Life

For Abigail this was a time of reconstruction and reorganization in her life, just as it was a healing time for the nation. The open sores of the bloody four year war were still in her psyche. But in the North she could see that industrial complexes were sprouting up like mushrooms. Industry began to replace the farm made goods that she had made at home. Looking out the window she imagined some of the gadgets that she saw in the general store back home, like the can opener, and reading about strange machines and products like the internal combustion engine, linoleum, rubber dental plate, and the first antiseptic surgery, along with weapons of war, like the Gatling gun, Dynamite, and the torpedo.

Abigail was being swept up in her rebirth and a Renaissance in New England. The large cities at the time like Boston, Philadelphia, and New York expanded and innovated to accommodate the influx of immigrants.

As the stage coach traveled south the mountains became smaller until they were riding next to hills and low lying roads that were near fast running streams and rivers. The streams congregated among the mossy bosses of the rocks. The Naugatuck and Housatonic rivers hugged the high hills as they orbited around them and dropped back down into the fast moving torrent.

While she was getting comfortable she became embarrassed with being with so many strangers. She dipped her chin down into her chest, crossed her arms and then closed her jacket closer around her shoulders.

One road that they passed through was deep below the exposed roots of the trees. For miles the flesh colored roots hung by the side of the road. The grey birch, elms, oaks and majestic spruce trees blushed with embarrassment to have the human animal look up their skirts as the carriage rushed by. The eyes of the trees stared down at the travelers. The trees pressed their bare roots close to the bank of the road and tried to hide their nakedness.

Factories began to crop up as they got closer to the coastline. The rivers where the manufacture's lifeblood, just as the blood of a human being keeps his body alive, these tributaries kept the hearts of the industries alive. Every manufacturer had at least one waterwheel grafted to the sides of their brick buildings.

She had read that these factories that they were passing by made many manufactured goods; clocks, pins, and guns were the products of the Naugatuck Valley, along with lamp fittings, cartridges, shoe tips, corset studs, wire chain, and a thousand other items stamped out of brass sheet or twisted out of wire.

She recalled that the town of Waterbury, with a population of ten thousand inhabitants and the next town that they passed through, made clocks in the industrial town that rivaled the timepieces in Switzerland.

They descended into valley towns like Ansonia and Abigail could hear the thump of the machines, even over the clatter of the wagon wheels as they passed by. Finally after a three hour drive they came to Noroton Heights where the Fitch school had been opened not more than a year ago.

She had read about Mr. Benjamin Fitch, and knew he was a millionaire who made his fortune with a chain of dry goods stores. He raised and organized the 28th regiment to go and fight the war. Then he later built the Fitch Home for orphans of soldiers who died in the service. The home cost 100,000 dollars and it stood near the corner of Noroton and West Avenue. This would be Abigail's home for, what she hoped, would be a long time.

"Everybody out that's getting' out," the driver said. Then the driver's helper opened Abigail's door pulled out her foot warmer and placed it at the path that led up to the Fitch building. Little wisps of smoke floated up and out of the tin container and into the afternoon air. The bottom of the warmer sizzled in the snow.

All her luggage was piled at the beginning of the lane. She stood there with her lap blanket being held in front of her while she watched the stagecoach drive away and heard the driver yell; "Ha my pretties, pull!"

The school was a paradise. In the background was the Long Island Sound. In front of her were ornamental shrubbery, flower-beds and many beautiful tall spruce trees that towered over the property. The statue of a seated Calvary officer embracing his daughter, sat in front of the property surrounded by well manicured round hedges. It was sculpted by Larkin Goldsmith Mead specifically created for the school. The snow seemed to cradle everything with its soft fluffy hands.

She was overjoyed, because there was nothing like arriving at the place that you thought you knew and finding that it was more wonderful and exciting than you imagined. Her belly tingled. Her baby shifted in her womb, which she took as a good sign.

The front door opened up and a tall dignified lady in a red wool Garibaldi shirt and a plain checkered skirt waved to Abigail. "Hello honey. Are you Abigail Armstrong?" She hollered from the door.

"Yes ma'am, that's me."

"Good."

An instant later two beefy men dressed in overalls came out and grabbed all her luggage and brought it inside. Abigail followed close behind.

As soon as Abigail got to the front door the woman said; "Welcome to the Fitch's Home for Soldiers, my name is Constance Davenport. I'm happy to know you." She held out her hand. As soon as Abigail shook her hand Constance pulled her close, then hugged her and whispered in her ear; "This is your home now dear." Then she held Abigail's arms high above her head and looked at her pregnant belly. "How far along are you honey?"

"Three or four months I think."

"Don't you know?" Constance narrowed her eyes and shook her head in annoyance.

"No not exactly."

Abigail changed the subject. "Do you have a young negro girl with the last name of Washington?'

"Oh no she left a long time ago and I don't know where she went," she said. "Let me show you around," she led her through the building.

As she followed Constance around the building she was disappointed that Daniel's sister had moved on. She hoped that she would meet somebody that she had something in common with. In spite of that, while she walked behind her she had great expectations for her new life.

The first room they walked into took Abigail's breath away. Constance walked in front of her and Abigail was so struck by the opulence of the room that she knocked into the padded seat in front of the piano. She caught herself when she slammed her hands onto the keys of the piano. The baby grand rang out a few sour notes.

"Are you all right my dear?" Constance asked.

"Oh… I just tripped. Thank you."

"This is the library and sitting room." She walked a little more into the center of the room and paused in front of the shelves of books. "These books were bought by Mr. Fitch and he personally stocked the shelves so everybody could enjoy them."

As Abigail walked over the parquet floor she stared up at the shelves of books that reached to the ceiling, it seemed to her that she was walking in a dream. The chandelier with the curved arms and small white shades smiled down at her and it thought how naïve this farm girl was as she walked below it.

The book shelves were of reddish-brown mahogany.

She passed a white padded couch that had a marble end table next to it and approached the ladder that was on wheels which was leaning up against the shelves. Even above the ladder there were more books on the second floor of the room. Her knee scraped against the silky smoothness of the padded couch with the claw-like feet and rounded arm rests. The sofa rested just under the ladder.

The high walls made her feel insignificant. They were white and high. And next to the fireplace two long windows reached from the ceiling to the floor. They both had heavy silk fabric curtains hanging down from the top.

Abigail grabbed the ladder and rested her elbow on one of the steps as she inspected the volumes. "I've never seen so many books in one place in all my life."

"Mr. Fitch encourages all his teachers to read as many books as they can in between their duties," Constance walked over to the bookshelf and slid a thick red leather covered book from the shelf and turned the pages as she talked to Abigail. "You're welcome to borrow as many as you like."

The large world globe purred and caressed against Abigail's dress to pull her attention towards it. She spun it until Europe and Africa passed by, and the image of America came into view. "There we are Miss Constance." She pointed to a tiny spot in New England.

"You don't have to call me Constance. Connie would be just fine."

"Okay."

"Have you seen enough Abigail?" Constance started to walk out of the room.

Abigail stopped her in her tracks. "Connie, I was wondering what that painting is that is hanging over the mantle?"

A large painting of a New England dock and two huge square rigger sail boats dominated the wall above the fireplace. "Those are two of the ships that Benjamin Fitch owns, which go overseas to trade with the countries in Europe."

"Really?" She strained her neck and looked up at the painting. "Isn't that wonderful. It's like he's bringing some of the culture of Europe back to America."

"You know, he is a world traveler, with all the millions that he has there's no place he hasn't been." Constance's body became rigid and she crossed her arms and looked at Abigail with a superior leer. Then they went towards the dining room. "Follow me."

"Okay." Just as Constance left the room a delicate porcelain figurine of a ballerina dancing on point got Abigail's attention. She picked it up and caressed it in her hand. She stared at the pink dancer and she wanted to keep it because she had never seen such a magnificent fragile thing in her life. She put it in her pocket and then hurried to catch up with Constance.

It wasn't the thing that captivated her so much, as the idea of the grace that it represented which enticed her to steal it. She had never stolen anything in her short life but this was too much of a treasure to leave behind. She saw it as the embodiment of all those places that Mr. Fitch had been to in Europe and she wanted a piece of that adventure.

Constance pointed at the open space in front of her. "Here is our kitchen and dining room capable of serving four-hundred people." Abigail heard the clatter of people and the shuffle of dishes. Then she followed her down the long high hallway.

As they walked Constance pointed into each room; "this first one is for our tailor," it had yarns of material spread out on a long table. "This one is the barbershop," two metallic and leather chairs took up the center of the room. "And down there is the pool room." The table stood in the middle of the room with strong legs holding it steady. Abigail just barely peeked into the room because she had a hard time keeping up with Constance as she tried to absorb all that flooded her senses.

So many rooms. I don't know if I'll remember them, and where they all are, she thought. At that instant she became conscious that she was falling behind so she hurried to catch up.

Constance pointed up to the ceiling. "The rooms upstairs are the barracks."

"Is that where the men sleep?" She looked up.

"Yes, exactly." Then Constance scooted over to the window. She pointed with her long bony finger. "Across the parade grounds is the laundry and boiler room and next to that are the chapel and the hospital."

They passed by wide stair cases and vaulted ceilings and Abigail could hear the shuffling of feet, the squeals of joyful children and the clatter of pots and pans in the distance. Turning the corner, they doubled back, and reached the large dining room. It had long flat tables that ran around the edge of the room. In the center was a tall round furnace that had a slender smoke stack that went up to the ceiling and out to the roof. It felt warm and cozy in the large hall and the smell of beef stew floated in the air.

"Children!" Constance clapped her hands. "This is Miss Abigail Armstrong. She will be training to be one of your teachers. Say hello." All of a sudden the noise stopped.

"Hello Miss Armstrong." A shout from everybody rose into the air as they greeted her.

"Thank you children. I'm sure we will get along marvelously."

"Sit, have some stew. In my opinion it's the best stew ever made." Constance directed Abigail to be seated so she could sample the food. Then she shouted to a large women in a white apron; "Marie… bring our new teacher some stew would you?"

"Thank you Connie." After that Constance waved to the woman as she came out of the kitchen and pointed to the table in front of Abigail. She placed a French White Porcelain bowl in front of her. It was filled to the top with beef stew and it steamed in her face. She could see that everything was only the best food; the orange carrots, the green celery, the white potatoes, and the brown meat in its own gravy looked delicious. The hearty aroma was overwhelming.

Abigail took a bite of the stew. "It's wonderful Connie. It reminds me of the kind of excellent food I once had when I went to Delmonico's in New York."

"I've heard of it but never went there." She put on a jealous sneer as she turned away. "Don't dawdle Abigail. I have to introduce you to Jonathan Fitch. He is the son of Benjamin Fitch, your employer."

"Okay. Just one more bite," she said as she shoveled in another spoonful of stew and then finally dabbed her mouth with a napkin just before she scooted off after Constance.

Chapter13

She meets the son

She followed her through the scullery where pots pans and dishes were piled up on the counters and in the sink. Abigail could smell the soap powder and see the suds in the washbasin. Her feet moved as fast as they could in order to get past the place that reminded her of the worst chore she once had to do on the farm.

"Constance," Abigail shouted. She had lost sight of her guide and was in the middle of a large hall with ceilings that seemed to reach to the sky.

"In here deary." She followed the voice and it took her into a billiards room. It was dark and luxurious. High backed leather cushioned chairs surrounded the pool table and a series of three lights hung high over the green felt. It had six claw-like legs holding it up and was made of mahogany.

"I thought I lost you Connie."

"Here, sit. Jonathan wants to talk to you." Abigail sat with a satisfied plop as she watched Constance leave the room. It was getting to be tiring chasing after her. In the background she could smell the remnants of a pungent cigar aroma and no matter how she tried she could not help fall asleep.

"Abigail, Abigail wake up." She felt somebody shake her shoulder. She looked up through her watery eyes and saw a young gentleman. He was wearing an expensive beaver fur hat and a frock coat. In his right hand was cane.

"I'm sorry. The baby tires me out. Sometimes I fall asleep and don't even know it."

"That's all right Miss Armstrong. I understand." He took off his frock coat and hung it on a hook on the wall. Then he leaned his gold topped cane on one of the chairs and picked up a pool cue. He glanced over at her while shooting pool. The balls cracked into each other and the black eight ball made a barely audible thud as it hit the bottom of the pocket. Between shots he lit his cigar. The purple smoke filled the room.

"I want to be a teacher for your orphaned children," she said as she got up from the chair.

"Yes I know. My father was very impressed with your letter and wanted to get you to the school as soon as possible. He's away now on a trip out West but he'll be back soon." He stopped and held the cue stick in front of himself while he looked at her belly. "We'll take care of your delivery. We have two excellent midwives available when the time comes."

"Thank you. Thank you for everything. I know I'll be happy here."

He laid the cue stick on the table and went over to the corner of the room and summoned Constance back by pulling a bell pull on the wall. Abigail could hear the muffled chime of the bell through the ceiling. He turned to her and smiled ever so slightly "You are important to us. You are the first face the children see when they get here. It is so important that they feel comfortable. They've gone through some rough times after losing their parents in the War."

"Yes I know Jonathan. Oh…I'm sorry is it all right to call you Jonathan?"

"That's fine."

"I know what you're saying because I didn't know my parents either. I was adopted."

"It's like you were sent to us Special Delivery. You're perfect for the job. Welcome to the Fitch Home." He shook her hand. It was gentle but firm. Constance entered the room. "Thank you for coming so promptly Constance. Please show Abigail her quarters," Jonathan said.

"Follow me Abigail, I'll show you your new bedroom. It's upstairs." They went through the first library room again. It was the room that she stole the little figurine from.

While they passed through the room Abigail thanked God for the opportunity to return the small statue to the table. Her guilt gnawed at her gut so much that the delicate figurine became an anvil in her pocket after Jonathan welcomed her to her new home. She reached in and set the little ballerina back on the marble table at a full run, because she was trying to keep up with Constance. It wobbled and then settled down next to the lamp. As she looked back, she could have sworn that the tiny dancer waved good bye to her as she left the room.

It felt so good to make things right. For her, at that moment everything was right with the world. Why should I steal from my home, she thought.

Abigail labored up the wide carpeted flight of stairs. Constance was at the top of the steps, arms folded and foot tapping while she waited for her to get to the top of the landing. When she got to the top of the stairs she looked up at her and let out a sigh of relief. "Well I made it."

Then Abigail followed her down the long wide hall. Constance opened the tall door. "This will be your room," she said. "This room is specifically for sleeping. No books or papers or ink or anything else is allowed in the bedroom. Do you understand?"

"Yes ma'am."

"Get settled and I'll be back."

Chapter 14

She pulls a child up to the light

She wanted to get acquainted with her environment. The image of her otter friends back on the farm flooded into her head. She remembered how they smelled and washed their food and how they bobbed and weaved trying to get as much information about their surroundings. She felt the same way about this new room.

Abigail walked past the marble top table in the center of the room, and dragged her fingers over its smooth surface. Her dress brushed up against a small bookcase while she pulled out the shallow rectangular-looking box of the chest of drawers. She was disappointed not to find any clothes in the bottom.

Then she walked over to the washstand next to the four poster bed, poured some water into the basin and washed her face. After that, she stood in front of the full length mirror and took out the silver comb from the back of her hair, by situating a compact mirror in back of her hair so she could see it in the mirror in front of her. She plucked it out and dropped it on the table. She was surprised to see how much her belly had swelled up since the last time she stood in front of a mirror.

All of a sudden she heard moaning coming from the other end of the house. She walked out into the hall and turned her ear toward the darkness of the corridor. The moaning was coming from a room at the end of the hallway. Abigail tip toed her way to a closed room. She pulled the squeaky door open a crack and then looked into the dark room. It had only a small rope bed and a chest of drawer in it.

Under the bed was a skinny little boy curled up in a ball. He looked out and up at her after she opened the door wide. "It's all right son. I won't hurt you. Come out," Abigail said as she opened the door wider, letting in a shaft of light that sliced through the darkness. The boy scooted deeper into the darkness under the bed as if the light was a knife stabbing at him. Abigail could hear the scrape of his feet and his grunt while he tried to escape.

He began to bang his head on the leg of the bed and move his fingers as if he were playing an invisible piano. She kneeled down and poked her head under the bed, he never acknowledged her presence. He was in his own little underworld. She let out a deep sigh of frustration. "How am I going to get him out from under the bed," she whispered to herself. Right at that moment she reached into her pocket and retrieved her compact mirror so that she could pin up the hair that had dropped down in front of her face.

It was then that she noticed the boy pop his head through the rope bed and stare at her. It was the first time that he became aware that she was even there. Abigail looked at him and then looked back at the little mirror in her hand. The light being reflected off the mirror got his attention.

"Here you go son." She handed the compact to him and steadied herself on the cross beam of the bed.

He first put the mirror in his mouth to taste it. He wrinkled his nose and shook his head. "Yuck," he said. After he tasted it he noticed that it was a mirror and that he could see himself in the reflection. It was literally the very first time he had seen his image. After he opened the compact twenty or thirty times, he finally closed it and pressed it close to his chest as he rocked back and forth.

"Are you happy now son?" Abigail said kindly. She covered her mouth, shook her head and closed her eyes. She was so relieved that this little animal was happy now.

"Abigail, where are you?" Constance hollered.

"In here Connie." Abigail got up at a snail's pace and faced her.

"Oh. You found one of the special children."

"He does seem to be different."

"Yes. He needs individual attention. You won't be teaching these children now, maybe later after you have an idea how to teach normal kids."

"Oh… I didn't know."

"Would you do me a favor Abigail?"

"Of course. What is it?"

"Go into your bedroom and get me the bedspread off of your bed and bring it in here."

"Okay." She ran into her room and whipped off a white Whig Rose appliqué quilt that was covering her bed. She had it by one corner and dragged it down the hall. As soon as she got in the room she twirled it around like the cape of a matador and let it land open on the floor. "Is that all right?"

"Yes that's perfect." Constance spread the quilt out a little more with the palms of her hands. "Patrick, it's time to go home." After that she half lifted the boy up and placed him in the middle of the blanket.

"What are we doing?"

"It's the only way we can get him out of here, otherwise when he's alone he wanders off," she said. "Grab the corner of the cover and I'll grab the other side. We'll carry him down the stairs like this."

While they carried the strange boy through the hall and down the steps Abigail wondered if this was going to be how her days at the school were going to be and if she had made a mistake wanting to be a teacher.

Finally they got to a room in the back of the house. Constance knocked on the door. A woman's voice answered; "Yes who is it."

"Barbra, it's me Constance. Open up. Patrick wandered off."

All this while Patrick just lay in the quilt, motionless, except for the hold he had on the compact. It was so tight that his fingers began to bleed. It was then that Abigail realized he had broken the mirror and the glass was digging into his hands.

Abigail pointed to the boy. "We have to get in so we can bandage his hand."

"Oh my," Constance said.

Abigail heard the click of the bolt on the door slide open, after that Constance pushed against it with her back until they were in the middle of the room. She was astonished by a room filled with comfortable beds and toys. Among the clutter were the children. They were clean and dressed in the finest clothes any child could hope to wear. The boys were decked out in vests and white shirts and black ascot ties. The girls wore full length yellow and violet party dresses.

All the children paid attention to what they were doing and not to the other students around them. Several children drew pictures with crayons on the white walls. They were pictures of the yard outside the window. The pictures were like paintings; they were detailed and full of life, the trees and snow looked real, so real that Abigail could hardly believe that little children drew them.

She sat down while Constance and Barbara bandaged Patrick's hand. All of a sudden she felt a pressure on her shoulder. A little blond girl with rivulets of hair hanging off the back of her head and dressed in a purple play dress grabbed her. She suddenly wrapped her arms around her neck. The girl began to coo and sob.

Abigail pulled her around to the front and then she wrapped her arms around her. "It's all right Missy. Abigail is here. Don't worry."

Constance and Barbara stopped and stared at Abigail. Barbara spoke. "That's the first time I ever saw Jenny take to anybody, and I've been here since the school opened."

"I was just sitting here. I didn't do anything to make her come up to me," Abigail said.

"These children are special. They see and hear and feel things that we mortals will never know. She must have seen something in you that we evidently can't see. After you get your training you might want to consider teaching our special children." Then Barbara continued to clean and bandage Patrick's hand.

Chapter 15

The Training Begins

"Go Abigail. Get some rest. Tomorrow we start your instruction." Constance, with her arm around Abigail's shoulder, walked her to the door and closed it behind her. She heard the bolt slide shut.

After she got upstairs she stood in front of the window and watched the snow begin to fall with big fluffy flakes that coated the statue in the front yard. Men were out in the snow shoveling the walkways clean. It seems they always want it accessible. They make sure that the school's arms are always wide open, she thought.

She unclasped her arms and started to unpack her clothes when she came across the telescope and the two books that William had given her. She hung her clothes on hooks and folded her blouses and put them in the drawers. But where do I put the books and the telescope, she thought.

Just above the headboard was a lose plank. She pulled it open and stashed her precious gifts inside the wall and then pressed it back in place.

It was time for bed, so she shook the silver bed warmer to get the coals to heat up, and then slid it under the bed by a long handle. It smelled of hickory wood and coal. She lay down in the feather bed with the covers pulled up to her nose expecting to sleep but the excitement of the day and the anticipation of the sunlight hours nudged her awake. Before she knew it the crystal sun sent light through her frosted windows and alerted her that the day started.

"Abigail it's time to get up," Constance said as she banged on her door.

"Okay I'm up." She slid off the bed, took off her nightgown and put on a new clean blue work dress.

"Meet me at the bottom of the stairs."

"I'll be there."

Constance stood at the bottom of the stairs, holding her arms loosely behind her back, chest out and chin held up high. "Let's go into one of the vacant classrooms," she said. The perfume of excitement floated in the air as Abigail followed her to the room. Constance went through a fence, which separated the bench-like desks from the teacher's area. It was in the front of the classroom. She sat on a chair next to a small blackboard that was on tripod legs. "Sit in the desk. I put papers and a pen on it so you could take notes."

Abigail tried to sit in the little desk by putting her rear end on the chair first and then pulled her pregnant belly in with her but she just would not fit. "I think my baby belly doesn't want to learn anything right now." She laughed to herself when she realized that she had become too big to sit in a normal desk so she sat side saddle with her legs sticking out in the aisle.

"Here Abigail sit on this." Constance handed her a chair over the fence.

She sat next to the desktop so she could lay her papers on its lid in order to write her notes. "That's better." The scent of eggs and bacon frying in the kitchen wafted their way into the room and mingled with odors of glue, construction paper, crayons, and damp paper towels.

"You'll see the books on the desk that you are to use." Constance pointed with the slate pencil that was in her hand.

Abigail picked up Webster's Blue Back Speller, then a Bible and then the familiar McGuffey Reader. "Oh yes, I have them."

"Now these concepts are very important. Have you ever heard of a man called Pestalozzi?"

"No."

"His principles are deceptively simple but they have a lot to say about how we teach our children. Write this down. One, begin with the concrete object before introducing the abstract. Two, begin with the immediate environment before dealing with what is distant and remote. Three, begin with easy exercises or activities before introducing complex ones. Four, always proceed gradually, cumulatively and slowly."

"They sound really logical and to the point," Abigail said as she picked her head up from the desk.

"Remember this Abigail, this is education of the head, heart and hand, but which is led by the heart. It is authority that is based on love not fear."

"I could see that put into practice when you were handling Patrick." Abigail smiled but Constance showing no joy or humor just nodded her head.

"It's harder with Patrick than with the other children."

"Why?" Abigail waited for the answer but Constance kept quiet.

"When I get to know you better I'll let you know why," she said. "But for now let's just concentrate on our lessons."

Abigail wondered why she dismissed her question so quickly and why she continued going back to the tutoring without an explanation. She pretended to write something on the note paper in front of her but managed to steal a glance at Constance. Her bottom lip quivered while she looked up at the atlas above her head.

"Okay," Abigail said as she looked back down at her notes.

"Come up here so you can familiarize yourself with all the equipment."

Abigail opened the knee high gate and entered the Teachers area. She squeezed between the table and the piano and then picked up a stick of chalk and began to write her name on the blackboard. "Abigail Armstrong Teacher. That's me."

"Not yet Abigail. You still have a long way to go."

"I know but you'll help me get there won't you?"

"Yes."

For the first time she saw Constance smile. "You can call me Abby since I call you Connie."

"Okay Abby," she said. "Now get the World Atlas open so your students can see it."

Abigail found the long round stick with the hook on the end and reached above the blackboard, snagged the map and pulled it open. She smiled at Constance. "I'm short but with my long stick I can reach all the way to the other side of the world." Pride welled up in her heart. She turned her face to the ceiling and smiled at the open map.

Then she walked over to a small blackboard on tripod legs set to the side of the room, next to the abacus. She wrote in tall bold letters; 'Hello Students Welcome to Miss Armstrong's Classroom.' At the end of the sentence she snapped the chalk onto the board making the period. The blackboard legs collapsed under themselves and the slate board crashed to the floor. "Oh my stars and garters!" she said. "What did I do?" She still had the white stick of chalk in her fingers and her arm was frozen in mid air.

Constance shook her head. "Not so hard Abby."

"Sorry." She bent over and picked up the blackboard. Then she moved over to the abacus. The teaching aid was taller than her and had blue, white, black, and green colored balls suspended on wires. She flicked the little balls across the wire to the other side of the abacus.

"I'll teach you about that thing at the next lesson. For now go back to your chair and take these notes that I'm going to give you."

"Yes ma'am." She went back through the fence and took her seat.

"There are three principles you might want to know." This time she got up and went to the board. Constance wrote with lightning speed and accuracy, and even though it was quick every letter was perfectly formed; 'from the known to the unknown, from the simple to the complex, from the concrete to the abstract.' "If you use these, you can't go wrong."

"As I look at them I see what you're saying," Abigail said, while she chewed on the wooden end of the pen. "I saw that when I was a young girl on the farm." she pointed with the pen. "We saw the seeds and knew they would grow into that plant but we didn't know how healthy or how unhealthy the plant would be until it matured. And the simple pips buried in the ground became complex corn plants, tomatoes, apple trees, peach trees and any other kind of plant you can think of. She stared directly into Constance's eyes. "Amazing isn't it?"

"Yes Abby. These children are our little seeds. We have to nurture them so they grow into complex human beings."

"I'm ready for more notes ma'am."

"This stuff is kind of dry but they are the methods we use to teach. Number one; prepare the pupil to be ready for the new lesson. Two, present the new lesson. Three, Associate the new lesson with ideas studied earlier. Four, use examples to illustrate the lesson's major points. Fifth, test pupils in order to ensure they have learned the lesson."

"Oh I see," Abigail said as she absorbed everything on the blackboard. "Sort of ready, set, go."

"Yes, if you want to put it that way." Constance put the chalk back on a shelf on the blackboard and clapped her hands to get the chalk dust off. "Come with me. This is an important part of your training." Abigail trotted behind her and tried to keep up as she scooted through the house into a room that had a class already in session. Abigail could hear the teacher reciting a lesson just before they turned the corner and entered the classroom from the back.

The teacher was in her thirties and her hair was pinned up at the top of her head, and she wore a plain white Garibaldi shirt and a black work dress. She was reciting from the McGuffey reader. She pushed her glasses back up to her nose a few times as they tended to slip off as she read.

The black and silver stove sat in the front of the classroom with some of the children's lunch pails; silver, black, and red ones nestled under it. The front of the room had a blackboard on the wall, with a clock and bookcase to its right. The tick of the clock could be heard as she read the book.

The children, the boy's in dark uniforms with the white collars, and the girls, mostly dressed in dark or light blue dresses sat very attentive as the teacher read.

"I want you to observe how she teaches. Get a chair and sit and watch and listen."Abigail got a small child's chair and in silence and with awareness not to disturb the class, sat in it with her hands folded on her lap. Constance left through a door at the back of the room.

While Abigail sat there her stomach began to moan and grumble. She hadn't had any breakfast. She knew the kitchen was still open because she could smell bacon cooking and coffee brewing. "Excuse me ma'am, Constance told me to sit and observe but I'm just too hungry. Can I leave miss?"

The teacher walked to the center of the room. "My name is Elizabeth. You can call me Beth if you like."

"Well Beth, if I don't get something to eat soon I'm going to die." Guarded laughter and snickers came from the children when she complained of hunger pains. Beth, the teacher, stared into the laughing children, and in an instant they stopped.

"By all means. I can see you're pregnant. Woe to man or beast that gets in the way of a pregnant lady when she's hungry." They both laughed. "Come right back when you're done."

"Thank you ma'am."

After a few minutes Abigail sat at the end of the table closest to the kitchen. The same fat kitchen lady that served her the beef stew came towards her. "What can I help you with ma'am?"

"I really would like some breakfast." The big dining room was empty except for Abigail.

"I'll be back in a minute." She turned and left for the kitchen. When she came back out she had a plate in her hand filled with eggs and bacon and toast. "Here you go missy."

Abigail shoveled in the scrambled eggs and then crunched into the toast. She picked up the bacon with her fingertips and held it next to her nose for a second before she ripped off a piece and then closed her eyes in ecstasy. "Ah… ambrosia." She smelled the nutty aroma of the coffee and lifted the cup to her lips. "So good." At that second she felt the presence of somebody in back of her.

Constance stood stiff and authoritative, with her arms folded over chest and a stern expression on her face. "What are you doing here? I thought I told you to observe the class."

"Yes but…"

"There are no excuses. You have to do what I tell you to do. Do you understand?"

"Yes ma'am. But I was so hungry. Haven't you ever been pregnant before? It's like you're a ravenous animal especially when your belly is as big as mine." This was a vain attempt at humor by Abigail. She thought it would defuse the situation. But it only made it worse.

"Are you making fun of me?" Constance leaned on the table and looked straight into her eyes.

Abigail put her head down and began to cry. "You're being mean to me just like my stepfather was before I left the farm." She sniffled and slumped even closer to the top of the table. Her tail was between her legs just like the submissive dog in the pack. The alpha female had her just where she wanted her.

But all of a sudden Constance straightened up and sat hard on the chair next to Abigail. "Your parents were mean to you?"

"Yes. Only my stepfather." When Abigail looked up she saw Constance pull back and get a faraway look in her eyes.

"I'm sorry little lady. I'm just so anxious to give these abused children the best that, I get a little cranky when I see things going in the wrong direction."

"I won't let it go in the wrong direction, believe me."

"Yes I believe you. She chuckled. "We're both like these children more than we realize aren't we?"

"What do you mean Constance?" Constance's words were like a lightning bolt that pierced her heart. She pushed back the chair all at once and started to leave. Abigail got up and asked her not to go. "Sit, please. I want to know what's bothering you. We can't afford to be enemies, especially for the sake of these children."

"Yes you're right." She let out a long sigh, sat back down and settled into the chair. "From the short time I've known you I've grown fond of you because I can see that you are a person of integrity."

"Thank you Connie. This is where I want to be. This is what I want to be doing with my life."

"I can appreciate that Abby. I feel the same way about The Fitch School," she said. "I know that I can trust you, so I'm going to tell you something that nobody else knows." She reached out and grabbed Abigail's hands that were lying on the table. "Patrick's not just another special child…He's my son."

To confide in Abigail was above and beyond anything that Constance had done in a long time. She had buried herself in the school. She tended and nurtured the children and kept the secret of Patrick's birth deep inside. If Abigail hadn't come along she would have carried the guilt and shame inside of her like a dead child in her womb.

"Oh, I know how hard that was for you to tell me. Thanks. Your secret is safe with me."

"I think he's the way he is because God is punishing me."

"What are you talking about? Why should God punish you?"

Constance got up and walked a few steps away from the table. Then she turned back. "The school is for orphans, not for children that have parents. Don't you think I should be punished for that?"

"No. Patrick is being taken care of. Where else could he get the attention that he needs, except here?"

Constance rested her hands in front of her and stared out the window, deep in thought. Then she talked in a monotone, as if her emotions had been stripped away. "The snow is deep and inviting like a fluffy white quilt."

"Yes. We ought to take the children out so they can go sledding."

"Now that I have you in my confidence, I have to tell you something else. It's why I'm sure God is chastising me."

"Go ahead tell me why?"

"When I was a child I was rebellious and never listened to my father. To be honest with you I hated him. Everything he told me to do I just did the opposite. And he was so mean to me. He beat me with a willow branch and would make me stay in the barn all night, and wouldn't let me out, until I was willing to do what I was told. He said, 'if I was going to act like an animal I might as well sleep with them until I came to my senses.'"

"Yes." Abigail listened without even turning her head. She was transfixed on Constance's story.

Constance stood rigid and rubbed her wrists as she rocked back and forth. "They used to lock me in the privy with my bible and told me to 'absorb God's words. Maybe that would cleanse my soul.' I didn't read it. I used it as a seat on top of the privy bench. Mom would slip me bits of food through the half moon opening. Most of the food pushed through the opening I couldn't eat because of the stink in there. You know, I never did read that bible, just sat on it."

"And that's why you think you're going to Blazes?"

"Yep. They always liked my sister Miranda best. They kept saying that she was prettier, had manners, and she could learn faster than me. They stressed all the time that she was smarter. I guess that hurt the most because I knew I was smarter than her."

All of a sudden Abigail got up, feeling embarrassed while she grunted and groaned as she stood up; her belly was weighing her down. She rushed into the library. She looked around for any bible on the shelves. At the end of the room next to the window and just under the world globe was a row of bibles. She grabbed two of the books and waddled back to the cafeteria.

"Here you go Connie." She handed her one of the bibles. "One for you and one for me."

"Okay now what?"

"Do just like I do." Abigail put the bible on the chair and then sat on it.

"Oh my God what are you doing Abigail?" She said. "Do you want to be dammed?"

"No, that's not going to happen Connie. It doesn't hold any magical powers. It's just a book."

Constance pulled out the seat across from her and sat down with the bible in her hands. "How can you be so sure Abby?" She opened up the book and flipped through the pages. "There's a lot of powerful stuff in here that I don't think I want to go against."

"Okay Connie."—she reached under her left cheek and pulled out the bible and slammed it on the table—"I didn't get struck by lightning did I?"

"No," she said. "But I think I'll play it safe for now. Maybe later I'll be able to do that."

"I understand Connie. It's hard to get out from underneath all that abuse that you had as a child. We carry that baggage around with us and it gets heavier and heavier the longer we hold on to it."

"The children here have a lot of baggage too." She sat up straight and a twinkle came into Constance's eyes. "Say, let's have the children and the soldiers in the barracks next door get together and have a sledding party."

"That sounds great!"

Chapter 16

With the Help of Angels

It was dark by now, after the children had been gathered up and the soldiers were picked off of their beds. The torches lit up the sides of the buildings and sparkled in the crystal white paleness of the landscape. Shadows of giants and angels jumped and flew across the white mounds of snow.

The soldiers sat in the small wooden sleds with children all around them like little sprites, waiting to do the veterans bidding. The warriors fidgeted and waited to be pushed down the hill. They were covered up in blankets and shawls and underneath their covers the twitch of half an arm, or half a leg, or the spasm of a nub, where a hand used to be, plagued the soldiers as they tried to sit still.

Abigail and Constance sat in the big one horse open sleigh covered by lap blankets and quilts to shield them from the cold. They watched the soldiers, as the children ran beside them. They slid down the hill only to come back up and slide down again.

Abigail turned to Constance. "I know how vulnerable it makes you feel when you tell me your secret." Abigail sipped her hot chocolate while she looked into the crowd of children and soldiers.

Constance turned her head. "Did I make a mistake confiding in you?" She asked. "Is my secret safe with you? After all I don't know that much about you."

"Of course." Abigail rested the hot chocolate on her lap. "Maybe you'll feel better if I tell you one of my secrets so we can feel equally indebted."

"Yes, that's a good idea."

Abigail knew that the less people were aware of what happened back at the farm with Burton the safer she would be. But in her heart she also recognized the fact that Constance made the first gesture of trust. On balance, they were both victims of the world of men and this action on her part would weld them together.

"If I tell you my secret you won't think the less of me and stop me from becoming a teacher will you?"

"No. We're sisters now."

"I killed somebody. The man was going to kill my future husband. He, like Lawrence saw the elephant which I think made him crazy. It was self defense, nothing less, nothing more."

"You killed… I can't believe it."

"It's true as tragic as it was. He was a bad egg and would have shot both me and Lawrence if I hadn't stopped him." Abigail could see that Constance was moved by her confession. She shivered and turned away from her. It was the cold frankness of the admission that grabbed hold of her and took her breath away.

Constance turned back, but this time she talked to Abigail's chest. She avoided her eyes. "Man alive! You sure can tell secrets. You got mine beat by a mile."

"So are we even now?"

"Yes." She turned back towards the crowd of people milling around down at the bottom of the hill.

Abigail was scared that she had done the wrong thing by telling about the Burton incident except she saw by her reaction that it was too late to take the confession back. If she could have pulled the words out of the air and stuffed them back in her mouth she would have done it.

Mean while, the children screamed with joy and the veterans laughed, possibly for the first time since the end of the war. Red faces, wet pants, and wet gloves became the medals that the sprites carried with them as they trudged to the top of the hill as they pulled the cut up soldiers behind them. All the veterans were in one man dog sleds, and tied in, so they could sit while they went down the hill.

There was a child on each side of them. The soldiers held on with one hand on the arm rests and one hand on the rubber sheets that they sat on. Sometimes even before they got to the bottom of the hill they would tip over. In that case the children would pick up the soldier, scarcely bigger than the students because of all the amputations, and place him back in his little chair on the sled.

Smiles cracked the faces of the veterans as they reached the top of the hill. Hugs from the children made them whole again. Some of the soldiers had no arms so they nuzzled into the chests of the little fairies. It became a mid summer nights dream, as far as the warriors were concerned. It was a night they would never forget, as long as they lived. For that matter, it was also a memory that the children would take with them as they grew up.

The angels bent over close to the bearded faces of the fighters and tipped cups of hot chocolate towards the lips of the Yankees that had no arms. They sat motionless and content. Their faces were flushed by the cold and underneath all that was the color of gratitude. Their eyes filled with tears which washed away the red color of war and allowed them to focus on the virgin white of a peaceful snow. They had given enough pieces of themselves for the cause, it was time to rest.

At the bottom of the snow covered hill there was a sudden crowd of men and children.

"What's going on down there?" Constance asked.

"I don't know Connie," Abigail said as she pulled down the blanket off of her shoulders.

"Please go down there and see if everything is all right. Those Billy Yanks aren't quite civilized yet. They might be teaching our children something raw and uncouth like gambling or spittin'"

"Yes ma'am. I'll do just that." Abigail got off the sleigh and walked back into the school and through the classrooms and kitchen, until she came out at a door that opened up next to where the students were playing. She opened a gap in the door so she could hear and see what was going on outside.

John Chapman, a soldier with a severed left foot and an amputated right leg, was sitting comfortably in the wooden sled barking out drill commands to a line of kids with wooden broom handles on their shoulders.

"Attention hut," he shouted. "Right shoulder arms." The children, like obedient recruits, marched in place, shoulders slung back and broom handles held high on their shoulders. "Right," he barked. With that the students turned their heads to the right. "Front," he said. All of a sudden everybody turned their heads to the front. "That's fine Blue bellies. At ease." The child at the end of the row collected all the broom handles and stacked them against the side of the building. Then they spread their legs and put their hands behind their backs.

Abigail swung the door open little by little, before she went outside, so as not to disturb the little soldiers standing in line. She wanted them to keep their dignity and pride.

"That's it soldier," Abigail said. "They've been trained enough."

"Oh, where did you come from?"

"I came out of that door." She pointed quickly. "I'm a teacher at the school." She walked next to the children, hugging herself against the cold.

He chuckled. "I'm not teaching them how to play poker or faro or introducing em' to a strumpet."

"You better not," she said. "I'm bringing the kids into the school now."

"What's your name? Mine's John Chapman."

She glanced back as she went through the door; "Abigail Armstrong." She was a mother duck with her ducklings following close behind all in a row.

His stares made her nervous and flattered at the same time. It was obvious to her that he looked beyond her fat belly and was interested in her as a woman.

She smiled to herself because in her chest she felt a sense of pride and purpose, and the independence that teaching gave her. It opened a whole new world. It pushed aside the life of drab labor and isolation. To open the world like a book and reveal the secrets of nature, this was the path that she knew she had to follow. Suddenly she got a cramp in her womb. "Ow, my stomach hurts." Abigail clutched at the wall in the hallway and then slumped down in a chair that was in her way.

A student walked up to her. "Miss Armstrong are you all right?"

Her mouth was open and her brow was furrowed with pain. She held out her palm in front of her. "Yes son, it's just the baby growing, I think."

"Should I go get Miss Davenport?"

"Yes honey. Hurry." He scooted away and came back in just a minute. He followed close behind Constance.

"Abby what's the matter? You look so pale."

"The baby reminded me that it's still there."

"Yes, they have a nasty habit of doing that once in a while." She turned and faced the children. "I want you students to go into the classroom near the cafeteria."

"Yes ma'am," they all said in unison, just before they left.

"When the time comes for you to have the baby make sure you tell the midwife that you want Chloroform. When I had it, it was only ten years in use. When you're in pain 'it's the sweetest smell you ever smelt.'"

"I'm feeling better now Connie. Maybe I should go back to the children?"

"No. I want you to rest for the remainder of the night. And then in the morning if you feel better you can go back to work."

"Why are you so good to me? You're like the mother I never had."

"I may be like the mother you never had but you are like the sister that I wished I had. Maybe if I had a supportive sister, my father wouldn't have been so brave shoving me around with two of us against him. We could have watched each other's backs, but as it was, my sister was my parent's favorite. Nothing she did was wrong"

"Is that what you're doing for me, watching my back?"

"You got it sister. We're in a man's world, and they're not willing to give us a hand."

After that Abigail retired to her room.

Chapter 17

Question Everything

The morning came and Abigail stretched her arms above her head and smiled to herself as she greeted the day. She got up and went over to the wash basin, washed her face, combed her hair and arranged it by sticking a gold hair comb on top of her head. Then she took a wash cloth and cleaned her belly and squeezed out the extra water into the basin.

"Well, Miss Armstrong it's time to teach," Constance said to Abigail as she stood in the doorway.

Abigail jumped. "Oh Connie! You startled me. What are you saying?"

"It's time to throw you in the pool. Either you sink or swim." Constance smiled and chucked. "Don't be afraid, just use your imagination. I left a teaching schedule on the desk."

Abigail followed Constance to the same classroom that she gave her the instructions in the previous day. The students were already in the room when she entered it. She slid between the desks sideways until she got to the front of the room, opened the gate and then sat at the desk. She expected Constance to be right behind her but instead she was still at the back of the room.

"Hello class," Abigail said.

A strong voice came from the back of the room. "Greet your new teacher children," Constance demanded.

"Good morning Miss Armstrong." All their voices were in harmony as they welcomed her to her new classroom and the beginning of a new life.

Teaching was the least of the chores that Abigail had to do. There was a paper on her desk that outlined her responsibilities; 1. Teachers each day will fill lamps, clean chimneys. 2. Each teacher will bring a bucket of water and a scuttle of coal for the daily' session. 3. Make you pens carefully. You whittle nibs to the individual taste of the pupils. 4. Men teachers may take one evening each week for courting purposes, or two evenings a week if they go to church regularly. 5. After ten hours in school, the teachers may spend the remaining time reading the Bible or other good books. 6. Women teachers who marry or engage in unseemly conduct will be dismissed. 7. Every teacher should lay aside from each pay a goodly sum of this earnings for his benefit during his declining years so that he will not become a burden on society. 8. Any teacher who smokes, uses liquor in any form, frequents pool or public halls, or gets shaved in a barber shop will give good reason to suspect his worth, intention, integrity and honesty. 9. The teacher that performs his labor faithfully and without fault for five years will be given an increase of twenty cents per week in his pay, providing the Board of Education approves.

Constance nodded ever so slightly to Abigail as she left the back of the classroom. Abigail was alone now with the eyes of the sixty children staring at her with expectations of something new and exciting.

She could feel her knees get weak and she could hardly breathe but this was no time to be timid, she had come too far to give up now. She opened the drawer in the desk and pulled out a box of pencils and a stack of paper. "Here, give everybody a pencil and a sheet of paper." She pointed to a boy in the front row. "Here, hand these out."

"Yes ma'am." A boy in a front desk came up, and then after that he distributed the pencils and paper.

Her voice went up an octave and she kept clearing her throat as she handed out the supplies. "Now children, these are magic pencils. I want you to put your name and age on the top of the papers and write as much as you can remember about yourself. And this is the magic part of the pencil. If you forget any details just put the pencil up to your forehead and you will start to remember again."

This would be her way of getting to know who the students were and how their past lives had influenced them. She knew that many of these students were abused in some way. The windows to that abuse had been closed off but she was bound and determined to open up their minds to the future and to heal their past.

While she sat there many of the kids put the pencils up to their foreheads, and then with a wide grin and a sparkle in their eyes, they at once began to write again at high speed afraid that they would lose the thought. Her little game worked and it would help her penetrate their closed past lives. She had a warm feeling course through her body and she let out a deep gratifying sigh.

***

Augustus, a ten year old boy with curly brown hair put the pencil up to his head and then began to write; when I was five I remember not answering my father fast enough one day, because I didn't hear him and was excited about going outside to play. I was always happy to be outside. I remember being shut up in my room for two days and getting only bread and water. Daddy said, 'it was the only way to break my spirit so that I would listen.'

Ann Taylor, a little blonde girl with pigtails and blue eyes, coped with life by staring at things for hours on end, pressed the pencil flat against her head and frowned trying to remember. Then she began to write in earnest. I don't remember mommy and daddy to good but I do remember being whipped for dirtying my frock, and being whipped when I cried or disobeyed, and being whipped if I tumbled down the stairs.

Todd Wells, a tall boy of twelve that only just fit in his desk, licked the point of the pencil, looked around, and then thumped the end of the pencil between his eyes as he lowered his head down towards the desk. He muttered and rubbed the back of his neck before he began to scribble on the paper. The only thing I really remember Miss Armstrong is my relatives teasing me. One day my mom and my aunt had a wonderful fancy cake and pudding on the table just waiting to be eaten. They said; 'sit and have a piece of cake and some pudding.' Just as I was going to enjoy the sweets they came and whisked them away untouched, saying that I couldn't have any sweets ever again because they were intended for the poor. Every time we have desert I feel sick and can't eat it because I remember what they did to me every time we had supper and cake.

Barbra Miller, a dark hair girl with glasses, sucked on the end of her pencil before she began to write. I lived in New Haven and when my father and then my mother died I was brought here. Mom and Pop never hugged me or showed me that they loved me and told me that it would have been better if I had never been born. When the people came to get me the woman hugged me and it felt so good that I cried. Please Miss Armstrong don't punish me like my parents did. When Mom taught me, if I made a mistake she would rap me over my knuckles with a ruler. I can never remember her ever caressing my hair or patting me on the back for doing a good lesson.

Nicholas Graves, a short stocky boy of nine tapped the pencil against the desk until all of a sudden he began to write. My grandfather took care of me before I came here. He said to me all the time, 'my daughter has always obeyed me so now it's your turn.' He threw my toys into the fire and told me to reach into the fire and get them. When I got burnt and started to cry he locked me in a dark closet all night. I hope there's no dark closets in the classroom Miss Armstrong.

"Do the magic pencils help you students to write and remember?"

"Yes Miss Armstrong." Little voices came thru the scratching sound of the pencils of sixty students.

"Five more minutes and then hand them up to the front of the class." All the children that were done with their assignment sat with their papers propped up in front of them as they read what they had written.

The frustration in the room was so thick that it was like an invisible anxious fog that hung over the children. Some wrote as quick as they could, afraid that they were not going to have the time to tell their story. And yet others, with heads down on the desks, scribbled so hard that their pencils broke, worried that they would be left behind.

All this time Abigail sat content and patient and waited for their declarations of independence from their abusive pasts.

A boy in the first seat in the first row lay down his pencil and looked directly at Abigail. "Miss Armstrong," the boy said quietly. "We want to know about you. Why don't you use a magic pencil and tell us about yourself?"

At first, she was taken aback by the boy's suggestion but the more she thought about it the more she realized that it was only fair for her to write about herself. After all they were entitled to know who was molding their minds.

"Yes you're right… by the way, what is your name?"

"Emile ma'am." Then he got up and placed his pencil on her desk. "Here, you can use mine. I'm finished."

Abigail became anxious just like the children. What should I tell them? How much should I tell them? She thought. She started off telling how she loved growing things in the garden and how she loved her little otter friends in the pond next to the farm house. How she realized that she wanted to be a teacher and how she wanted to start growing children just like she grew plants. And, the most important fact of all, which was that she, like them was an orphan too.

She pinned the paper on the wall next to the door so that the children could see it as they left the room every day. This was her badge showing that she had the authority to teach them, and she hoped that it would convince the children that she was one of them.

All the papers were in a pile on her desk.

She looked at the pile of paper on her desk and smiled. "Now that we have introduced ourselves, I would like to tell you what I want in my classroom." She said this while she walked back to her desk and when she got there she turned and faced the classroom. The students were stiff and defensive. Some of them crossed their arms, while others glanced at the clock, expecting the same old rhetoric about how the teacher wanted complete cooperation and unquestioning obedience.

But instead they got an unexpected, refreshing new set of rules. A wave of attention spread through the students and they sat up straight and listened to every word. "We are here to learn from each other. You may think that because you are children that you have nothing useful to say, because you've been told to be seen and not heard, and that I won't listen, but you are wrong. Each one of you has a story to tell and each one of you, being an individual, sees the world differently. And we, the student body, want to hear what that vision of the world looks like. My primary rule in our class is this; question everything. Let nothing go by until you are satisfied that you have the answer. Be like Socrates, question. Weed out the contradictions' until you have arrived at the ultimate truth."

Abigail went and pulled down the map of the United States. After Missouri, Minnesota, Iowa, and Arkansas there were large swathes of land undeveloped and wild; Kansas Territory, Indian Territory, Nebraska Territory, Utah, New Mexico, and Washington Territories. "There is a lot of land still to be explored," she said as she looked up at the map. "This is where we live. This is what our nation looks like."

A hand went up in the crowd of children. "Miss Armstrong."

"Yes."

"When do you think men like Daniel Boone will open up those wild places?"

"Men and woman will be compelled to blaze trails just because of the fact that it's wild and unexplored. There's something in us that makes us open Pandora's Box."

A girl with long braids and a blue ribbon in her hair from the back of the room stood and asked a question. "Ma'am, what is Pandora's Box?"

Abigail sat on the edge of the desk and stared out the window as she recalled the Greek mythology. "Pandora was a woman, now that I think of it; she was more like a girl that was told not to open a magic box because it would release different evils into the world." Then she looked straight at the class to make her point. "Lo and behold she opened it."

Abigail paused and turned around and faced the blackboard. "Now let's get back to our lessons for today." She hoped and prayed that the seed of curiosity that she planted in their little minds would grow.

"But…what happened next?" Because the children had to know, a universal shout from the students rose up to the ceiling. Everybody joined the chorus. "Yeah… what, what. You've got to tell us."

Their questions were music to her ears. With a puffed-out chest and a cocky radiant smile she whispered to herself. "It worked. They had questions." Then she turned back around to the class.

Their insistence kept up. "We have to know."

"When this first woman opened the box, disease, pestilence, and war came out and plagued mankind forever," she said. "But Hope also came out which was the salvation of the world."

"Women. They cause a lot of trouble Miss Armstrong."

"Not all of them. There was an Indian woman named Sacagawea that led the Lewis and Clark expedition all the way West. She could speak Shoshone so her translations helped the group communicate with the Indians." She rubbed her belly as she talked. "And even though she was pregnant and then later delivered her son she traveled with them with a baby in her arms."

"I didn't know that Miss Armstrong." The boy embarrassed beyond words slumped down in his seat.

"Her Indian name meant 'full of mischief and Joy.'"

A girl's hand went up in the back of the classroom. "Miss Armstrong we usually read from our bibles along about now."

"Fine, thank you for reminding me. But first I have to give you the rules that we will follow in the classroom; 1.Respect your schoolmaster. Obey him and accept his punishments 2. Do not call your classmates names or fight with them. 3. Never make noises or disturb your neighbors as they work. Be silent during classes.4.Do not talk unless it's absolutely necessary. 5. There shall be no lying, cursing or swearing, calling of names, fighting, wrestling, boxing, knocking off of hats or caps in time of play or at school but you should play agreeably, one with the other-the girls by themselves and the boys by themselves. 6. Bring firewood into the classroom for the stove whenever the teacher tells you to. 7. If the master calls your name after class, straighten the benches and tables, sweep the room, dust and leave everything tidy. 8. The teacher shall be obeyed in all things."

The same little girl raised her hand again. "Can I read from the bible?"

"Yes you can missy, but I want you to read some passages that we will talk about later," Abigail said. "Write these down; Ecclesiastes 7:12, Proverbs 16:16, Proverbs 14:13, Deuteronomy 11:19, Proverbs 18:15, Proverbs 9:9, and Daniel 1:17."

"I have them," she said.

"Now read the Proverbs first, then go on to the others."

"Okay," She fingered the pages until she got to the passages. "Proverb 7:12 for wisdom is a defense, and money is a defense: but the excellency of knowledge is, that wisdom giveth life to them that have it. Proverb 16:16 how much better is it to get wisdom than Gold! And to get understanding rather to be chosen than silver. Proverb 4:13 take fast hold of instruction; let her not go: keep her; for she is thy life. Proverb 18:15 the heart of the prudent getteth knowledge; and the ear of the wise seeketh knowledge. Proverbs 9:9 give instruction to a wise man, and he will be yet wiser: teach a just man, and he will increase in knowledge."

"Thank you, that will be all for now. You can sit down," Abigail said. "Deuteronomy 11:19 is one of my favorite passages as it says that children are in the minds of educators and in the minds of people that care about them. And Daniel 1:17 where they talk about how knowledge and skill was given to the children, especially Daniel for he had the understanding of all visions and dreams."

Todd Wells raised his hand. "Should we take everything from the bible and use it like a textbook?"

"No son. Please listen carefully to what I'm about to say. The bible is a good book to show us how to conduct ourselves and guide us through life but it is just a book. We will be taking our knowledge from the Blue Back Speller, the McGuffey Reader, Webster's Readers' Assistant, Elements of Geography, and A New Guide to the English Tongue."

There was a murmur in the crowd of students, and Abigail knew that the whispers and mumbles that swept through the children was a sign of their dissatisfaction and confusion. For the longest time all they knew about learning came from the bible, and she also knew that that practice had to stop.

Their knowledge, as far as she was concerned, was going to come from their touching and seeing their environment, and asking questions about what they saw and what they couldn't see but could only imagine.

"That sounds good to me school marm." The squeak of the wheels of the soldier's wheel chair could be heard as he turned it towards the front of the class. "Do you remember me ma'am?"

"I remember… John Chapman right."

"Yes. I was wondering if I could stick in the back of the class so's that I can get some learnin.'"

"Sure soldier, I don't see why not." All the students turned their heads to the back of the room.

"I really like what you said about questioning everything. Maybe if I had questioned my orders I still would have my foot and leg."

"I don't know about your particular situation but I'm sure you're right. Oh, by the way, John, I was wondering if you still had your back pack from the war and if you would be willing to show the contents to the students?"

"Sure ma'am, I'll go get it right now." He all at once turned his chair away from the class in the direction of the hallway. A big smile came over his face and color flooded his cheeks.

"No John. Tomorrow would be soon enough."

"Aw, I was looking forward to showing it to the class today."

"Okay if it wouldn't be too much trouble, that would be fabulous." She said. "Class." Abigail clapped her hands to make the students turn back around and face the front of the school room. "Open your bibles and start to read Genesis until John gets back." The shuffle of feet and the turn of pages could be heard as the children settled down to wait for a glimpse into the world of a soldier.

It was only ten minutes and the squeak of his rubber wheels from the wheel chair could be heard coming down the hall.

"Here I am," he said as he wheeled up to the front of the room. The pack was nestled on his lap. "Here you go." He handed Abigail the pack and then started to wheel away.

"Hold it John; I want you to tell us about what's in the pack," she said. "As I take the object out you can tell us about it. Okay?"

"Sure." He sweat and swallowed hard because he was the center of attention and he wasn't use to it.

Abigail opened the pack and put the contents of it on the table.

John reached over and picked up each item and started to describe it; he opened up his draft notice, put it on his lap and smoothed it flat against his good left leg. "I kept this paper because I was so proud to be in the Army and to be helping the cause." He picked up his toothbrush. "I whittled this out of a branch of hard wood and drilled the eighty-eight holes for the hog's hair bristles."

"Did the Army give you what you needed?" Abigail asked.

"Yes ma'am. They did pretty good in given' us what we needed but some things we wanted to have to remind us of home," he said. "I even brought my sisters bible with me and put it in my pack, don't ask me why, I can't read."

Abigail interjected. "You can't read?"

"No ma'am. Can't hardly understand a single written word." He stared at the table, trying not to look at her eyes. "Can sorta' write my name a little.

"We'll take care of that."

"You mean that you can teach me to read?"

"Yes john. Take a McGuffey reader with you for tonight and look at the pictures. Tomorrow I'll answer any questions you might have about the book."

"Thanks ma'am." He took the book and put it in his pants pocket and then turned back to the things in his pack. "The skillet, the tin cup, and the steel plate seem to go together." He clinked the three together as he picked them up. "We boiled and fried with them and kept that cup close, hooked on our belts so's we could scoop up water from a stream or a well."

"And where did you put your food?"

"I put my food; my coffee, my canned salt pork, and my rice, and the hardtack into the haversack. Then I stuffed my knife, fork, and spoon in there too."

"What about your clothes?"

"Didn't have that many clothes. I had my sack coat, my cotton shirt, my blue trousers, my Kapi, my U.S. belt and buckle, and my Brogan's." He picked up one of the boots and stared intently at it. "Guess I'll only need one of these, now that I only got one good leg." Then he threw the boot back on the table.

"I'm sorry about your leg, John."

"That's okay ma'am. Just left parts of me back on the battlefield. Some of the boys is still there. I guess I got away lucky."

"Anything else that you can tell us?"

"No, guess that's about it, except I still had a mirror, cards and dice, lye soap, candles, my housewife and a few sheets of paper and a pencil in the pack too. Couldn't write but I sure could draw. It worked pretty good. My canteen, I usually carried slung over my shoulder and next to my side.

Chapter 18

Friend or foe

"I'm ending class for now, so that you can go and eat your breakfast," Abigail said to the class.

The students filed out of the room in neat military lines. Each row marched out as the next row waited its turn. In no time, the entire classroom was empty and the desks stared at the couple as they shielded their emotions from each other.

The only people left were John and Abigail. John's wicker and wood wheel chair creaked as he lowered his chin to his chest and fidgeted in his seat. His words were hard in coming because of his embarrassment. "I didn't mean to interrupt your class Miss Armstrong."

She turned her back to him while she erased the blackboard, and cleared her throat, and politely reassured John that he hadn't done anything wrong. Her action bordered on the edge of being rude. "No, that was all right. We learned a lot about what you carried in your pack and what your life must have been like."

"The only thing I didn't show you was my Spencer Carbine which I paid ten dollars for when I left the Army of the Potomac."

"How are you coming along with that wheel chair? Are you getting the hang of it?" By now she had turned back around and was clapping the chalk dust off of her hands.

"When I first got the chair I couldn't stand it." He pulled and pushed on the wheels while he talked. "I wanted to throw it off a cliff because it reminded me every day that I was crippled. But after a while I tamed this wicker monster to do whatever I wanted it to do. Now, I can make this chair do tricks." He pushed the chair forward fast and then leaned back so the chair balanced on the wheels, and after that spun around until he suddenly fell back to the ground.

"That's really something John," she said. "Please don't hurt yourself."

"Oh, don't worry. This wheelchair is part of me now," he said. "You want to see another trick?"

"Okay."

He propelled the wheelchair so that it sped down the hall. When he got to the end of the corridor he turned and pushed on the wheels as hard as he could, which made it come back towards the classroom. The squeal of the rubber wheels echoed through the hallway as the chair skidded to a stop and then flipped over onto its side.

"Oh my God John. Are you all right?" Abigail rushed over but could not pick him back up because the combined weight of him and the chair was too heavy. She stood over him unable to help since he was unconscious. She bent down and shook his shoulder; "John wake up."

"Wha… What happened?" He blinked his eyes and grabbed Abigail's arm. "Guess I went too much like greased lighting."

"Can I help you back into your chair?"

"No that's all right. I can manage." He slid out of the wheelchair and then pulled it upright. Next, he plopped his rear end onto the leg rests and then bounced up to end up in the seat. The chair drifted back, as if it had a mind of its own, until he got control of it. "There we go." He let out a long sigh of accomplishment.

"Please don't do that again. You scared me to death. I thought you broke your neck."

"Sorry Miss Abigail. I won't try that anymore."

After that Abigail and John went to breakfast.

While she sat with the teachers, Constance came up behind her and whispered in her ear. "When you're done I would like to have a word with you in the parlor Miss Armstrong."

She turned her head. "Yes ma'am right away." A teacher across from her reacted with a guarded smile. After she had finished and was walking towards the parlor she wrinkled her brow and bit her lip all the way to the living room. 'What have I done now,' she thought.

Constance sat in the big high backed chair when she walked under the entrance to the room. Her stern look startled Abigail so she kept her distance and hung out near the fireplace.

"Question? Question everything? Do you know how dangerous that is for a child?"

"No I don't know." The challenging tone of the question made Abigail sit hard in her chair.

"When we deal out discipline, don't you think that the children will question our punishment?" She leaned forward.

"Possibly. If they think it's not fair."

"Then who's to make the final decision whether it's fair or not? Certainly not the child."

"Yes I agree with you. Not the child. That is our responsibility. But for everything else, especially at that age of innocence, there must be an open forum for questioning."

"For everything else?"

"Yes Constance, everything. How else can we learn? How else can the children learn?"

"I can't allow you to teach our children in that manner. I want you to take more control of you class or I'll replace you. Do you understand?"

It was as if Constance had reached into her chest and had a hold of her heart and had squeezed the life out of it. Abigail just stared at her for a minute.

"Yes I understand," she said. "Connie, can I ask you a personal question?"

"Of course."

"If when you were a child and were being abused by your father, as you told me, and had questioned what he was doing, do you think he would have continued?"

"Yes I think so. And I probably would have gotten beaten worse."

"Then you know how powerless you felt, and how alone you were. We have an opportunity here to not beat our children if they ask questions. Work with me. Don't let these children have the door slammed in their faces. Let's keep the questioning alive and well, by letting them ask everything they want to know."

Constance got up from the chair and went over to the fireplace, closer to Abigail. She stared into the hearth and whispered to herself; "yes, I would have gotten beaten worse." She turned to Abigail with tear filled eyes. "Okay you win, but be careful."

"I will."

After Constance left the room Abigail thought about the fact that she was a product of an age that was slowly melting away. Constance was a representative of the middle class in America, and because of it, she demanded that the old rules of society be obeyed. Abigail felt that she was being pressed between two worlds; one dying and the other being born.

She looked at her hands and reminisced about working on the farm until the sun went down. Now her hands were used for shuffling papers and correcting assignments. And she knew that her self-education and her reading of books is what got her the job and not her connections. It was not a matter of who you knew but what you knew. The rural ethics was a thing of the past. And now all that mattered was a person's education and abilities.

Even though she had high expectations for the career, the fact remained, that there was harshness to the profession. She saw now, that the image of the teacher was considered as a lowly job without much reward. The pains in her back demonstrated that teaching was physically hard and the work demanded long hours in the classroom.

As it happened, the position paid poorly, despite the fact that she was employed by Fitch. And besides all that, she was expected to be an example of a morally upright citizen. She knew that there was whispering among the teachers, as to the fact that Abigail's husband was nowhere to be found, which brought into question her moral standing.

But to her way of thinking it was better to be a teacher than to work on the farm as a slave to Noah. There were many times as a teacher, that she had to clean the hearth, and bring a heavy scuttle of coal to the stove, and fill the lamps with oil for the school session. She carried not only the wood and coal but the weight of her baby as she did her everyday jobs.

Back in the classroom, Abigail sat silent and pensive for a while until she sensed that the class was ready for her lecture. "Now that you have all had your breakfast and are fully satisfied I'm going to tell you a story and after that I want you to tell me what you think about it?"

The students satiated and full sat and waited to hear what this new teacher had to say. They leaned forward, and some of them rested their chins in their palms as they stared at Abigail.

She looked out at the class and then began. "Let's say that an old ugly man began questioning how the government was treating its population. Let's say that he was complaining about the lies that the heads of the government were giving its citizens. And let's say further, that the men in charge didn't like what he was saying. Do you think they have the right to do away with him?" she asked. "Go ahead somebody answer, don't be afraid."

There was a long pause and nobody had the courage to raise their hand, until, way in the back of the class, a lone arm bit by bit went up in the air.

"Yes," Abigail said.

"My name is Todd Wells ma'am." He got up and looked like the cowlick on the top of a head of hair. He towered over the students around him while he leaned to the side. "If the government is helping him in any way and he isn't doing what they say, they have the right to shut pan his mouth." Then he sat down quickly. The desk slid on the floor scraping along as he plopped back into it.

"To kill him?" Abigail asked. There was a lot of mumbles and the shuffle of feet but nobody replied. "Oh come on children, somebody must have the courage to give me their opinion. Remember, I won't hold it against you. What you say in the classroom stays here."

A girl in the front row raised her hand and then stood up. "Ester Rollins ma'am." She squirmed and looked down at her desk. "I don't think they should kill him just because he was asking questions."

"Then it's our right to ask questions no matter how uncomfortable it might be to the people in power?"

"Yes." She looked up at Abigail while she slid back into her desk.

Abigail felt that her message had gotten through, so now all she could do was to wait and hope that all the negative education about not questioning anybody or anything, would be replaced by her positive instruction about not settling for a pat answer.

Chapter 19

The Light of the Cave

Abigail had ended the lessons in the Blue Back Speller and the students were finished for the day.

John sat silent in the shadows of the room.

"John…I didn't know you were still back there. You gave me a start."

His heart beat a little bit sadder thinking that she was scared of the image of him in his wheelchair. If I was a whole soldier and standing up tall I bet she would be happy to see me, he thought.

"Sorry Miss Armstrong didn't mean to frighten you." He said. He wheeled up the aisle and threw the McGuffey reader on her desk. "Man alive! I couldn't make heads or tails of this book." It was a hard thing for John to admit, for he wanted so very much to impress her.

"That's all right Mr. Chapman. As soon as we teach you the alphabet you'll start to know what this book is all about."

"Would you call me John?"

"Okay. John it is."

Suddenly Constance came running into the class. "Abigail, Patrick is missing again. Please help me find him." John backed his chair into one of the desks.

Abigail and Constance left as if a devil was hot on their trail.

John sat and stared into the emptiness of the room. All of a sudden a force deep inside of his gut grabbed hold of him and pulled him through the hallways as if a giant magnet had pulled him to the edge of a precipice.

He sped out of the classroom, through the kitchen and into the parlor. Abigail ran past him and went up the stairs. Constance followed close behind and he could hear their feet through the ceiling as they ran from one room to another. The sound of beds and furniture being shifted around in the bedrooms echoed through the ceiling.

Abigail descended the stairs and passed by John. "Did you find him yet?" John asked.

"No. We're going down to the cellar. Constance told me that they found him down there once."

"Can I help?"

"No, that's all right." She rocketed past him, and only just paused enough to let him know what had happened. She disappeared into the darkness of the underground rooms.

His heart ached and the sad feeling that rumbled in his stomach suddenly exploded. He clenched his fists around the wheels until they turned white. He lowered his head and dropped his shoulders. He just sat there for a while and stared into his lap. "I'm going to help whether they like it or not," he whispered to himself. He followed her to the edge of the landing, and looked down at a staircase that disappeared into the darkness of the basement. His palms started to sweat and his lip quivered but he was ready to try, even though it might mean a painful fall down the stairs.

He slid down off the wheelchair and scooted over to the edge of the top of the landing, and then plopped his rear-end on the first rung and leaned back towards the chair. On each successive step he slid down and at the same time dragged the wheel chair after him until finally he reached the bottom of the stairs. He gave a long sigh at the bottom and got back in the chair.

He could smell the odor of fresh oil paint and then realized that it was coming from the stack of paintings leaned up against the stone wall. The smell of the dank underground room made him light headed.

He passed by many marble statues; The Pieta, The standing David, and Venus de Milo. They were as foreign to him as the man in the moon but he marveled at their beauty. The room was filled with art objects. But the one that mesmerized him the most was Venus de Milo because she had no arms. Even as he wheeled by, he gazed at the statue until it disappeared into the darkness.

He could hear the two women scuff their feet over the dirt floor in the distance and see the flicker of their candles. "Abigail… Constance…Where are you?"

"We're here. Just follow our voices."

As he wheeled up to them he said; "I'm here to help."

"Who helped you?" Abigail asked, surprised to see him.

"Never mind that, just tell me what's going on." He leaned forward, looked up at the women, in anticipation of giving them something they least expected from a cripple; a helping hand.

"I found Patrick down here between these large vases and bronze statues once." Constance said. "But he's not around here now." She sobbed and clenched her hands and paced back and forth.

"What's that?" He asked. He pointed to a small wooden door hidden behind one of the vases. It was half open.

"I don't know John. I've never seen it before," Constance said. "It looks like it goes right through the wall and into an opening behind it." She opened the little white washed door and looked past it, and then shoved her candle into the aperture behind the entrance. "It goes down below the basement." The door was painted the same color as the white walls so that it would blend in.

"Could that be an underground railroad hiding place?" Abigail asked. She bent over and looked into the passageway.

"You're right Abigail, that's what it is," John said.

 Constance pointed at the hole in the wall and then moved about unable to settle in one place, as she wrapped her arms around her chest because of the damp cold air in the cellar. She fixed her attention on the escape route. "Do you think

Patrick could have crawled through there? This house is close to the seashore and only eleven miles away from Wilton where there is an underground railroad," she said. "This could have been a 'way station' and the Fitch family could have been 'agents' for the slaves."

John slid off his chair and opened the little door and peered down the dark passageway.

"I can't crawl through there because of the baby and Constance is too big. What are we going to do?" Abigail asked.

"Let me have one of the candles, I'll go in there." John took the candle out of Abigail's hand.

The light flickered and danced off the walls of the crawlspace. The walls were made of field stones and the space was about three feet high and four feet wide. This one instance was an advantage for John because half of him had been donated to the Cause.

He made slow progress as he scraped along the sides of the walls and slid over the rocky floor. While he slithered down the little opening a field stone dropped off the wall and plunked to the floor. John was afraid the whole structure would collapse on him.

Half way through the cave a voice echoed through the tunnel; "John, are you all right?"

"So far so good," he turned his head and shouted back down the tunnel. His voice slid through his frosted breath. The cold of the cave was getting worse the farther in he went. In front of him was a carpet bag barring his way down the rest of the route. "I found something."

"Is it Patrick?"

"No. It's a carpet bag with some papers in it." He jammed the candle into the dirt, opened the bag and pulled out a letter and began to read it. The paper crackled as he unfolded it. The note was written in pencil and the message was full of hope and explicit instructions;

Dear Abraham and Cecelia;

This letter will give you the key to your freedom. If and when you get to the Fitch House approach one of the servants and say to them, 'We're here to go down the river Jordan,' they'll know what you mean.

After that they will show you the way to escape to Wilton and then to Farmington Connecticut. Remember, follow the Big Dipper (the drinkin' gourd) and the North Star, they are your highway to freedom.

Your Heavenly 'Conductor'

Samuel Holt

After he read the letter he stuffed it back in the bag and shoved it back down towards the entrance. He could see that the escape route stretched out in the distance, but only as far as the light from the candle could reach, then it became a black hole.

It got colder as he wiggled closer to the narrow exit of the tunnel. He began to shiver but pushed himself forward because he expected to see Patrick any second. But in the back of his mind the pesky thought that the boy didn't crawl down this hole at all, kept pinching at him.

At last he came to the end of the cave. Above him was a trap door. He pushed it up and it opened. His hands stung and he blew into them to keep them warm. The inky black sky with all its sparkling stars greeted him and the most prominent of all was the Big Dipper that pointed to the North Star.

By now the candle had burnt out and there was no light except for faint starlight. "Patrick…Patrick are you out here?" John shouted. No answer came back from the darkness.

While he scanned the trees for any sign of the boy he was startled by a hand on his shoulder. He turned and there was Patrick with a big grin on his face. "You're it," he said.

"Boy am I glad to see you. Come over here." John grabbed him and pulled him back down the hole, he pushed him ahead so that he could nudge him along down the length of the passageway. "Constance," he shouted. "Light some candles at the entrance so we can see where we're going."

The muffled reply came back. "Okay."

John pushed and prodded Patrick along by poking him from behind. They had to avoid rocks that had fallen off the walls. John's heart beat hard against his chest and he wanted to scream. He kept an eye up at the walls expecting them to collapse in on them. At long last, they reached the entrance of the Underground Railroad. Along the way he picked up the carpet bag.

A Teacher gets Taught.

Chapter 20

After the drama of finding Patrick had faded away, Constance was eternally grateful. She showed her gratitude for helping find her son because she left Abigail alone to teach the way she saw fit. It turned out that her kindness helped Abigail's cause along more than Constance knew. The children found that a new and exciting world had opened up to them. No longer would they be 'seen and not heard,' or ignored and abused. They wanted to know; they wanted to question, they wanted to open up every door that was closed and Abigail's teaching gave them license to do it.

In the back of the room in the shadows, as inconspicuous as he could make himself, was John. Not only the children had become excited about learning but he had replaced his preoccupation of being in a wheelchair with his eager longing to learn how to read.

Everything seemed to be going along fine until one day while sitting across from Constance, Abigail learned just how crass and common the teachers thought she was.

"A lady doesn't use her knife to spear her food, you know," Constance said. "It is customary to gather the food around the fork and use that utensil first."

"Oh, I'm sorry. I was never taught how to be a lady, just how to pick vegetables, not how to pick my food." Abigail placed her knife and fork on her plate and folded her hands together and positioned them between her thighs. She sat there just staring at her plate.

"What's the matter Miss Armstrong lost your appetite?" Constance asked.

"All of a sudden I just don't feel like eating. It must be the baby." She became withdrawn and still.

After everybody had left Abigail sat alone at the dinner table. Beth, the first teacher she had met came up to her. "Remember me?"

"Oh yes. Elizabeth right?"

"No. Call me Beth."

"Okay Beth."

She came over and rubbed Abigail's back. "You're not alone. Lots of people have a hard time figuring out what fork or spoon go where. Most of us here, the teachers in particular, have come from well to do families and have been taught the fine art of being a lady. It's pounded into us as we grow up."

"I guess that's where I lost out. I came from a farm. I'm not a fine lady just a farmer's daughter."

"Don't minimize where you came from Abigail. It's one of your greatest assets," she said. "After all Mr. Fitch saw something in your letter that he liked."

At the same time that Abigail looked up at Elizabeth she pushed her plate aside. "Will you teach me how to act like a lady?"

"Of course. I'd be delighted to." By now the dining room was empty and Elizabeth wanted to start right away teaching Abigail the finer points of how to eat at the table. She ran into the kitchen and came back out with a handful of knives, forks, and spoons and a ceramic plate. The plate and the eating gear clattered as she placed them in the center of the table.

Abigail had no idea what to do with these foreign tools piled in a heap in front of her. They looked like tools that a doctor might use to perform a delicate operation. Elizabeth began to describe the utensils and how they were to be used; "On elegant tables each plate or 'cover' is accompanied by two large silver knives and a fork for fish, a small fork for fish, a small fork for oysters, a large tablespoon for soups and three large forks," she said. "The napkin is folded in the center of the plate with a piece of bread in it."

Abigail looked up at Elizabeth with a dazed look in her eyes. "How am I going to remember what goes where when I start my meal?"

"Oh, don't worry about that. All this stuff will be set up before you get to the table."

"Wow! I have to be a surgeon to eat." They both laughed.

"As the meal progresses the knife and fork and spoon which have been used are taken away with the plate. And remember the fish should be eaten with the silver knives and forks."

Abigail smiled to herself as she rearranged the silverware on both sides of her plate. It takes a lot of manners to be a lady. Is it worth it? She thought. She decided that yes it was worth the effort because it was her ticket to becoming the teacher that she always wanted to be. "Is that it?"

"No Abigail. Remember how you were using your knife; well it comes into play for sweetbreads, cutlets, roast beef or other organs that have to be sliced, but for croquettes, rissoles, Bouchees a' la Reine, timbales, the fork is always used."

"When we sit down to an elegant meal will you shoot me hints across the table so I don't make a fool of myself?"

"Sure Abigail. Better still, after I show you everything I know, take all of this stuff up to your room and practice on your bed."

"That's a good idea. But I hope Constance doesn't catch me practicing."

"Why?" Elizabeth leaned on her palms as she looked into Abigail's eyes.

"She said that the bedroom was only to be used for sleeping and nothing else."

"Oh don't worry about her. Since she's been here she's turned into an old biddy."

"Well let's continue with your lesson. After dinner you must see that everything is cleared off the table before the dessert-plate is put before the guest. They must have a gold spoon and a silver desert spoon and fork."

"Okay."

"Let me tell you about how to eat fruit."

"You mean that there's actually a way to eat your fruit?"

"Oh yes, if you want to be seen as a lady; Take the strawberries by their green stems in your fingers and dip them into the sugar. Pears and apples are peeled with a silver knife and cut into quarters and then picked up with the fingers. Grapes should be eaten so that the grape seeds fall into the palm of the hand."

"When I was working on the farm I never dreamt that fruits would be handled so delicately."

"It's all for the images of appearing to be like a lady. Sometimes I get a little tired of the entire pretense too. But it's what the men expect of us. I think it makes them feel more masculine when they see us as frail and delicate."

"How long have you known how to act like a lady," Abigail asked as she shifted from casual conversation to a pointed question.

By now Elizabeth had sat down. She fidgeted in her chair and became rigid. "Gee… I guess all my life, ever since I was a little girl. All of the women here were taught just like me, from a young age to act as we do."

"I'm so far behind. I'm afraid I'll never catch up."

"Don't worry so much about trying to fit in Abigail." Elizabeth grabbed her arm to make a point. "You're just right the way you are. For now, learn these silly rules, if it makes you feel more comfortable, but don't forget the lessons you learned from the farm. They are much more valuable."

"I'll try," Abigail said. After all that was learned from Elizabeth, she was surprised that she denounced everything that she had just taught her as 'silly.'

Then Elizabeth got up and looked at the ceiling trying to remember some more manners that she could impart to Abigail. "Oh, the knife and fork are both used for eating salad. A very small spoon is served with the coffee. A half ladleful is enough for a bowl of soup. Only put half of the spoon in the mouth. To put it all the way in is impolite. I guess that's it."

"Thank you. I've learned a lot from you and nobody will ever get the idea again that I'm not a lady."

"When we're at supper and I see that you're doing the wrong thing, I'll just give you a glance to help you along, okay," Elizabeth said. "Nobody will see. They'll be too busy trying to be prim and proper to notice."

"That's a deal," Abigail said and then shook Elizabeth's hand hard and firm like a man would do when he struck a pact with another man. She imagined both of them spitting on the floor after closing the deal.

After her instruction she would spend many hours practicing the skill of eating like a lady at the dinner table by using the stolen plates and silverware from the kitchen. The dishes and cups would clink against each other, and Abigail would glance down the dark hall, to make sure nobody had heard her practicing her lady-like art on the bed.

When she was done she would put them in a blanket and stuff them under the bed so that she would have them for the next lesson.

At dinner, Elizabeth would frown when she picked up the wrong fork or used the improper spoon. And other times would clear her throat when Abigail in an unseemly fashion started to spear her food with her knife.

All the meals from then on were not an embarrassment to Abigail. Even though she mastered the art of the dinner table she knew deep down inside that she was not up to the sophistication of the other ladies in the school. Beth helped her jump over the obstacle that separated her from polite society, all though she knew that there was still dirt under her fingernails.

Abigail was happy to have another friend at the school, but as to Constance being her friend, she came to the conclusion that that friendship was over. The reason could only be, that she was afraid of me revealing the secret that I had about Patrick being her son, she thought.

Constance tried to keep her distance from Abigail. She would nod to her respectfully when passing or acknowledge her presence; "Good morning Miss Armstrong," she would say, avoiding any intimacy until one morning she corralled her in the dark hall that led to her classroom.

As she passed by, she grabbed her arm and swung her around until Abigail was facing her. "Yes, what is it Connie?"

Constance stood with her arms folded over her chest. "You're nothing but a dependant which has to be taken care of. You've never stood on your own two feet."

"Yes you're right. I'll get help from where ever I can so I fit in."

"Is that why you asked Elizabeth to teach you how to be a lady?"

"Yes." Then Abigail started to walk away.

But Constance would not let her leave without getting in a last jab. "You have no money and your family is just farmers."

"You're right again but I'm not ashamed of being a farm girl. It was a good wholesome life."

"How can you fit in? All the women here are from well to do families. You ought to be begging us to stay here."

"I belong. I was asked to come to the Fitch school by Mr. Fitch." Abigail stood for a minute and looked into Connie's cold eyes.

After that, Constance turned her back to Abigail and strutted away.

A sorrow seeped into her chest when she thought of her lost friendship but she still had her teaching to keep her company, and the enthusiasm of the children to brighten her day.

Chapter 21

The Sun Dogs

Many weeks later while Abigail taught the class an interruption opened up a new and exciting month, although a call by an unwelcomed visitor threatened to upset her joyful world.

"Turn to page seven in The Elements of Geography and learn what island, Gulf, Peninsula, Estuary and lake mean," Abigail said. "We'll talk about what they are as soon as everybody studies the meanings."

The sound of pages being flipped and the shuffle of little feet could be heard above the calm mood of the classroom. The simple uncolored pages showed the contrast between the island of England and its surrounding lands.

"Okay put your books down. Can anybody tell me what an Estuary is?"

Abigail pointed to a boy in the first row. He stood up to speak. "My name is Robert Bluebonnet ma'am."

"Yes."

"An Estuary is a body of water that empties into the sea." The boy glanced at the other students for encouragement and tugged on his lower lip not being sure that his answer was right.

"Good. Thank you," Abigail said. "Goodness… All of a sudden a cold wind rushed through the classroom. "What's that?" Abigail said as she got up and walked to the back of the room.

Two men in overalls opened the back door and had dragged a Balsam Fir through the hallway. The man with the rail road cap on and flushed cheeks turned to look at Abigail. "Sorry to bother your class ma'am but we were going to set up the Christmas tree in the parlor." He shook the tree and then buried his nose in the pine needles as he took a big whiff. "She's a beauty ain't she?"

"Yes it is. You didn't bother us." The pine smell of the evergreen lingered in the classroom long after the tree was out of sight. While she walked back up to the front of the class she wondered where the time had gone. And the smell of the tree brought back good memories of the pine trees on the farm that were cut down for the holiday. It's only a few days till Christmas, she thought. It was then that she was aware how important teaching was to her. The joy of education made the days pass by like having a good friend next to her on her journey through the winter months.

"Miss Armstrong. The fire in the stove is dying out. Do you want me to put in a few more logs?" A boy next to the wood stove was already walking over to the heater to put in some wood.

"Oh, yes. Please."

There was an aura of anticipation coming from the class while they waited for Abigail, who stood motionless, to give them the lesson for the day. But she was caught up in her own thoughts.

"Ma'am," Julie Hill, a little girl with black braids, woke her from her daydream.

"Thank you Julie. I was thinking about something else." She shook her head, blinked her eyes and turned her concentration back to the class. "Let's forget about our lesson for today and go and watch them put up the Christmas tree."

The class was a giant who woke, stretched and then clamored out of the room, anxious to stride through the hall and stand over the Christmas tree as it took root on the parlor floor. Laughter and whispers followed the students down the hall. They filled every nook and cranny except for the space near the fireplace, where the tree was to be set up.

Abigail stood in the back of the throng with her arms crossed and her attention on the two workmen who were putting the tree in the stand. The support was a round metal pot with four strap-like legs and two bolts running through the legs. It was surrounded by a miniature green picket fence. The fence was seventeen or eighteen inches square.

They tipped the tree to support it on their backs as if it were a drunken friend that they were bringing home to put to bed. It was thirty feet high and scarped the ceiling as they set it up.

They dropped it into a metal pot with a clunk and then they filled it up with wet sand. All the while one of the workers held the tree steady while the other one tamped down the sand around the base of the tree so that it would stand up straight. The squeal of metal could be heard as they tightened the long bolts which squeezed tight around the trunk. The men stood back and surveyed their work satisfied that their friend was safe and secure.

The dense dark-green tree stood tall in front of the fireplace. Its spire-like tip scraped the ceiling as the students strained their necks looking up at it. Its purple-green pine cones stood at attention on its branches, and clashed with the thin grey bark.

The children crowded around it and touched its arms and trunk. But this time the tree shook with joy to have the young hands caress its belly.

While Abigail stood there her students closed in closer and closer to her, until they invaded her personal space. At first she became uncomfortable but step by step she relaxed, resigned to the fact that she was becoming at ease in not moving at all.

And then it dawned on her as if a bolt of lightning had just struck her in the heart. These children need a mother as much as they need a teacher. They are from situations where there is no family and they are starved for human contact.

So she put her arm around the boy to her left and the girl to her right and pulled them even closer. Then she inched nearer to the girl in front of her with a nudge of her pregnant belly, until she had settled into the cocoon of students.

"Sirs," Abigail shouted. "Can we have a branch from the 'Abies balsamea' tree to set up in our classroom?" She walked through the children and up to the workers. They smelled like cold winter snow and pine resin.

"What's that?" The man stood there with a confused look on his face. "Abe…abe?"

"It's the Latin name for the tree." Abigail smiled and the students behind her giggled.

"Oh, isn't that curious," he said. "Sure, you can have a limb." He picked up his hand saw and grabbed a bottom branch and began to saw it off. The tree quivered as the steel teeth ate through one of its arms. It gave out a sigh of relief when the man put a dab of tar on the cut. He handed the tree's arm to Abigail.

"Thank you sir. You're so kind." Abigail buried her face into the pine needles and took a big sniff. Clean, fresh, and pungent were the words that came to mind.

The branch from the tree was put in a pail of sand and put on Abigail's desk so everybody in the class could see it.

The day had drifted towards late afternoon. When all of a sudden a boy from the back of the class blurted out; "Miss Armstrong what is that?" He pointed out the side window.

"It is not proper to interrupt the class by shouting," Abigail said as she got up and went over to the glass.

"But look." The boy held his arm up with his other hand and bounced up and down as he pointed with even more intensity.

While Abigail looked out the window the class abandoned their seats and surrounded her. "Ooos and aahs" echoed around the room.

There were amazing light pillars in the late afternoon sky. The sun shined bright just above a grey winter cloud. A pillar of light descended to the ground while the other shaft ascended above it. It was bathed in a brilliant halo with companion suns shinning hazily on both sides of the circle. I can't believe what I see. Are there three suns? See, see, they embrace each other like I used to embrace Lawrence as we kissed, she thought. Then she turned back to the class.

"They are ice crystals being reflected by the sun, children. It's nothing to be afraid of." She shaded her eyes. "There are three suns, one right next to the other and they are called sundogs."

"Is it a bad thing?" A boy asked standing next to her ear. "Will we have bad luck?"

"Oh no," she said. "As a matter of fact it's a good sign for the hunter. It is a blessing for a good hunt."

"But we're not hunters."

"It's not only a blessing for that. It also blesses the traveler on a quest for justice."

If she had known then what a letter contained the next day, she would have thought that the sundog was a portent to disaster instead of just an atmospheric anomaly. She dismissed it and went back to her desk and continued to teach the class.

The next morning a letter came that threatened to shatter her world.

Chapter22

Jonathan Helps

She noticed a letter on her desk as she was about to start her lessons for the day. "Children, turn to page twenty-five of your McGuffey readers and read the passage silently to yourselves."

After she was sure that her students were occupied she picked up the letter and became excited when she saw that the return address was New Athens Connecticut. She thought that it might be a letter from William Collins, the new worker, or a letter written by him for Daniel, so her Negro friend could say hello. But all her hopes tumbled down when she began to read.

New Athens Connecticut
December 20, 1865

Dear Mrs. Armstrong
Fitch's Home for Soldiers
And Orphans
Darien, Connecticut

I am writing this letter to inform you that moving out of the county without letting me know was against the law considering that I was still in the middle of my investigation and specifically instructed you not to leave. I doubt that you are telling me everything that you know. And since the body of the man has never been satisfactorily identified I will be pursuing this matter further.
I am not unaware of the impending holidays so I will be taking a trip to Darien in the spring, on March 20, at a time when the roads are passable.
I advise you to secure council if and when I visit the school. From all that I have seen in my examination it doesn't look good for you.

Sincerely Russell Dalton
County Constable.

She began to cry after she crumpled up the letter and slammed it on her desk.

A boy in the front row with a frown on his face dropped his book on his small table and whispered to Abigail; "Miss Armstrong are you all right?"

"Yes…yes go back to your reading. Everybody just keep reading." Her chair squealed against the wood floor as she got up and pushed the seat back with her rear end. Then she rushed out of the room and headed for Elizabeth's class.

She stood at the door and gazed through the glass pane at her friend while she taught her students. Elizabeth noticed Abigail and left the room and opened the door making Abigail move back to let her out.

"What's up Abigail?" Elizabeth closed the door and leaned on the wall behind her.

"I just got a very disturbing letter in the mail." She waved it in the air. "What will Mr. Fitch think when he finds out that a detective is coming to the school to talk to me?"

"Is that what the letter is about?"

"Yes, and the detective advised me to get a lawyer to represent me. I don't know any lawyers."

"Relax Abby. Jonathan Fitch is a lawyer."

"You mean the young man that I met when I first got here?"

"Yes. Go see him. He is here in his study. Go talk to him."

"Okay I will. Thanks. Oh, by the way will you look in on my class while I talk to Jonathan?"

"Yes, don't worry about your students."

She rushed off down the hall and in the direction of his office. When she got there the door was closed. She tapped with her pointer finger and then covered her hand over her mouth thinking that she might have disturbed Jonathan.

Suddenly the door swung open. "Oh… Abigail it's you. I wasn't sure anybody was at the door the knock was so faint," he said. "Come on in."

"Thank you. I have to talk to you about representing me," she said. Then she handed him the note. "It's about this."

The room was grand with the mahogany desk in the middle of the floor, with a high-back leather chair behind it. The walls were a continuing series of bookshelves stuffed with law books that surrounded the office and in the air was the persistent smell of the cigar that he smoked.

He went over to his desk and sat down and read the letter.

"Sit. Is this why you have to secure my services?" He held the correspondence in the air and then placed it on his desk before he lit his cigar. "Does the smoke bother you?"

"No."

"Are you in trouble?"

"Yes. But I'm afraid to tell anybody else because it might land me in jail." All at once Abigail got up from the seat and made for the door.

Jonathan got up from his desk chair. "Please Mrs. Armstrong sit back down and tell me what's wrong. I'm your Lawyer now. Do you know what that means?"

She turned around and eased herself back into the seat. "No I don't." A young country girl had no idea of the confidentiality of the client lawyer relationship.

He sat on the edge of his desk. "It means that whatever you tell me here, in this office, is privileged information. Nobody else need know what went on here."

"Oh, I'm glad to know that." She leaned as far forward as she could in the chair while she squeezed against the baby in her belly.

"I've got an idea. You tell me a hypothetical situation. A situation that is supposed but not necessarily true."

Abigail's eyes lit up because, even though she wasn't a lawyer, she understood the implications of just supposing but not admitting to the crime. "Suppose a man, a crazy man, was going to kill somebody that you loved and you killed the crazy soldier instead, killed him and then buried the body?" All of a sudden she began to cry and put her palms over her face. Her testimony echoed in her hands. "I can still see him in my mind when I think of that day."

"Did you fear for your life when this was all happening?"

"Yes I did." Abigail at last rested her hands on her lap while she stared at Jonathan. "I thought that after he tried to kill Lawrence that he was going to kill me, so I shot him."

"The gun? Who did it belong to? Was it both of your property? Did your husband give you the gun for your protection?"

Abigail had a faraway look in her eyes as she looked up at the ceiling. "Yes, he did mention that once."

"Aha, that's good. And who else knows about what happened that day?"

"My stepfather, Daniel, and Lawrence."

"But did anybody else actually see it happen besides you and Lawrence?"

"The Negro worker Daniel Washington."

"Do you trust Daniel to tell truthfully what he saw?"

"Yes absolutely."

After he heard her story, Jonathan picked up the cigar from the ash tray and relit it. He blew the smoke at the ceiling and then focused back on Abigail.

Abigail could see that he was deep in thought.

"Mrs. Armstrong. I have to ask you some personal questions. I hope you don't mind," he said. "Remember everything you say is just between me and you."

"Yes I understand," she said as she watched him get up and pace to the other side of the room.

He turned in her direction and paused for a second before he continued to walk towards her. "How pregnant are you? What I mean to say is, when are you expecting the baby?"

"I think I'm six or seven months along. I think it will be in February or March."

"Good… good. Don't have it any sooner okay?"

Abigail snickered. "If it wants to come sooner I won't have anything to say about it. Mother Nature tends to be a fickled mistress."

He cleared his throat and walked back to his desk, not looking at Abigail as he sat down. "Yes I can appreciate that. But it would be better for us if you were still pregnant when you took the stand to testify."

"Okay Jonathan I'll try."

"I was wondering where Lawrence is, do you know?"

"No, he left me and went down South to find himself," she said. "When he lived here he was very unhappy and jumpy."

"That will be all Abigail. Continue with your teaching and try not to worry so much about that detective. You're safe here at The Fitch School."

She got up and curtsied to him when she left the room but then stopped and turned back. "Thank you Mr. Fitch. You made me feel a whole lot better about that letter."

"I'm glad I could help."

After she closed the door behind her she put her ear to it and heard the rustle of papers and the turn of pages in a book. She assumed that he was hard at work on her case so when she walked down the corridor she let out a deep sigh of relief.

Chapter 23

They Dress up the Tree

When Abigail came back to her classroom her class was subdued and everybody had their heads in their books. "Thanks Elizabeth. Everything is better now."

"Good," Elizabeth said as she got up and patted Abigail on the wrist just before she left her classroom.

"Students!" Abigail shouted. "No more studying. We're going to dress up the Christmas tree." She went over to the students and organized them into groups. Each one had a specific decoration that they would make; paper snowflakes, paper chains, pine cones painted all different colors, popcorn strings with cranberries, small candles so they could be mounted on the branches.

The day carried on as the hum of the students filled the room and the sound of paper being cut and the swish of decorations being painted hung over the classroom.

Apples and nuts were being strung together and hung between the shinny foil strips. Gingerbread, hard cookies in the shape of fruits, stars, hearts, angels and bells lined the insides of the branches.

The most skill that was evident was little meticulous paper images of the teachers. Small Abigail, tall stately Constance, and round, kind faced Elizabeth hung on the end of the long green branches, and smiled out into the Christmas room.

Finally the tree was complete and illuminated by red, blue and white candles. The children stood back and surveyed their work. The ooh's and aahs floated through the air as the children admired their work.

"Now it's our turn," Constance said as she entered the room with a line of her students close behind.

"What do you mean Constance?"

"We have some glass Christmas tree balls hand crafted in Lauscha Germany. These will put to shame anything that your students have fashioned."

Abigail stepped in front of her. "How can you say that? Did you see how hard they worked on their decorations?"

"Yes. They're crude and unprofessional." She held the professionally made ornaments up in front of her. "These ornaments were made by German craftsman."

The students started to put on cute glass blown angels, adorable little children, and little elves. The final ornament was a Christmas ornament elephant hand-colored with various colors of glitter. It had embroidered ribbon and green beads, Silk fringe and red tassels were also added. A die cut Victorian girl was placed on top of the elephant. Constance cut the top branch and pushed on the ornament on the very peak of the tree. "There we go." She stepped back and folded her arms over her chest.

Abigail's students opened up a circle around the tree and with down cast eyes backed up as if they had been forbidden to breathe the pine air, forbidden to absorb the joy of their work, forbidden to watch the tree puff up with pride.

"Your ornaments are beautiful Constance but the children spent a lot of time making their works of art."

Constance sneered at the students. "They're hardly works of art Abigail." She walked up to a chain of multi-colored paper and flipped it up with her fingers. "Hardly works of art," she repeated under her breath.

The days became shorter and the snow started to fly and the animals that hibernated started to grow thick fur in anticipation of the long winter.

Even the human animals in the Fitch school felt a slight slowing down of their activities. Abigail noticed her hair grow thicker on the sides and thin on top but she attributed it to her healthy body and the reaction of the life growing inside her. Realizing that she was indeed slowing down through the winter months she wondered if she, like all humans, were affected by the snow and the lack of sunlight.

She looked out the window at the big fluffy snowflakes covering the sill and the deep pack of white that blanked the entrance to the school. Every day the blanket of white got thicker and thicker until it reached up to half the height of the evergreens on the front lawn.

In time the Woodchucks, ground squirrels and bats succumbed to the winter.

The Woodchucks heart slowed to four beats a minute, as he twitched and wiggled his body deeper into the pine needles and moss. Everything slowed. Even his teeth stopped growing while he slept. Occasionally he would get up to nibble on food, and to use its underground toilet room. And so the winter moved on for this underground dweller.

The bats gathered together one last time, turning the sky black with their numbers before they flew deep into the cave to spend the winter months, huddled up against each other for warmth. There were clicks and peeps mixed with the sound of their flapping wings. And likewise the winter moved on for these winged mammals as well.

The ground squirrel was curled up in a ball with its nose buried in its back paws and crunched into its pile of chestnuts which it used for its bed. The burrow held him in its hands and caressed him through the long nights.

Then there are the 'light sleepers' that take long winter naps just like the human animal trying to cope with the cold. The skunks, raccoons and the opossums that breathe a little more slowly and lower their body temperatures a few degrees while asleep.

The students like the animals of winter, nod in class and shiver against the wintry breezes that make their way through the open spaces in the wall. They try to wake their minds to the chalk lessons on the blackboard but the wind rattles the windows and the snow swirls off the roof which pulls their attention outside. They want to curl up like the ground squirrel and forget the snow.

A boy stares out the window and wishes he could be a snake, or a turtle, or a frog and imagines himself buried below the frost line in the mud so he could be snug and warm.

The children create a hibernating mass when they walk close and hug each other on impulse. They are imitating the animals of the forest, whether they are aware of it or not. Like the garter snake that hibernate with other species and are content snuggling up to a copperhead or a rattlesnake. The student's differences are put aside when they congregate together.

A bear snorts, growls and clicks its jaws as it slithers down a hole that leads to its den to 'lightly sleep' some of the winter away. It would awake now and then to forage or to give birth to its young.

And so Abigail took joy from her teaching as the winter pushed on and the lives of both human and animal was affected by the long cold nights and the short days.

It was March now and the icicles on the roof melted and made puddles in the deep snow, and like the bear in its den that gave birth to its cub, Abigail felt the life kick against her belly, determined to be released from its womb.

"Children…stay quiet and read your books while I leave the classroom." She held her belly and ran out of the room. "I'll be back." Then she went down the hall to Elizabeth's class and banged on the door. "Beth… it's time, she said as she doubled over onto the floor.

Beth opened the door, and as she did Abigail was pushed across the floorboards. "Oh, Abigail we have to get you to the midwife," she said as she lifted her up off the ground.

A few minutes later they rushed her to the midwifes' room. If it had been any later she would have had the baby in the hallway in front of Elizabeth's door. The bed was large with a mahogany headboard and a fluffy feather mattress. The room was in subdued light which bounced off the walls giving it a yellow glow. On the night stand was a container of chloroform with a small mound of gauze next to it. The difficult and sometimes dangerous experience was thrust upon the young Abigail like a bolt of lighting.

Abigail recoiled from the sight of the bedroom where she was about to give birth. But even more frightening was her terror about the possible death of her baby. She had heard about so many children dying during child birth.

A large German lady, called Lene Braun had learned her midwife skills in Germany when she was a young girl, no older than Abigail. She was a highly valued employee of the Fitch school.

She motioned to Abigail to lie down on the bed with her head resting on the feather pillow. "Ven you wake you vill have a beautiful baby to hold in your arms," she said. "Now breathe deep." She placed the gauze over Abigail's face and then turned to Elizabeth. "I heard other midwives say; 'the mothers should arm demselves vit patients, 'but I tink since we have dis drug, vee should use it."

When the drug was poured into the gauze Abigail imagined stars, clouds, and the man in the moon, as she saw it through William Collins telescope. The chloroform smelled like caramel candy, and for an instant she whirled around in her mind; it was a world of chaos and confusion then nothing.

And then; it seemed like an instant later she awoke to hear the sound of a baby cry. "Is that my baby?" She asked.

"Yes Abby, it's a boy," Beth said.

"Let me have him." She had woken up at 6 in the evening to see her son dressed in white. She touched her lips and her fingertips to his soft cheeks as she cradled the infant in her arms. "I'm going to name him Lawrence."

"That's a good name Abigail. It's too bad that your husband wasn't here to witness the birth. This is a valuable contribution that you have given him."

"Yes it is. And it's the only thing that I regret; that he wasn't here to see the birth of his son."

The nurse came over to the side of the bed. "Now, I vont you to rest for a while and then I vant you to get up and walk around." The nurse bent over and kissed Abigail's forehead. "You ver brave and you did a good job delivering the baby."

"Thank you ma'am."

The nurse patted her on the shoulder just before she left the room.

The baby cooed and squirmed in its tight swaddling blanket. Abigail disobeyed the midwife's orders to get up and move around; instead she fell back asleep with Lawrence suckling at her breast.

So, Monday, Tuesday and Wednesday passed; and on Thursday she finally got up and handed the baby to Lene. And now those three days had ushered in a new happiness in her life.

The morning had made a considerable difference in her existence. It brightened her day so much that it out shined any day that had come before it.

She went back to her regular routine of teaching class with Lawrence in his wicker basket on the floor next to her desk.

A girl in the first row tentatively raised her hand and then got up. "Miss Armstrong, my name is Nellie Carpenter and I would like to say something that all the students wanted to say but were afraid to."

"Yes Nellie what is it?"

"Well, we want you to know that we all admire you for coming back so soon to teach us, just after you had your baby," she said. "And we are so glad that you are our teacher."

"Thank you children." By now Abigail was sitting on her desk with tears in her eyes.

Nellie looked at the floor as she talked. "We kind of think you're like Sacagawea showing us the way even though you have a child." Then the students began to clap and they didn't stop until they saw Abigail crying.

She sniffled, and bit by bit lifted her head back up. "Thank you children. That's probably one of the nicest things anybody has ever said to me. I'm honored. We have to go back to work now children." She turned around and continued to write the spelling words on the blackboard. The chalk whooshed across the green slate board and then squealed and snapped at the end of the word. "Sorry about that children. Let me get another piece of chalk." Just as Abigail bent down to get another piece from her desk, a blonde hair boy interrupted the silence.

"Miss Armstrong, there are two men coming up the walkway to the school."

"That's all right. Just pay attention to the lesson." Again she turned back toward the board. She started to write on the chalkboard but all at once, she little by little turned back around and faced the window. She knew even before she had twisted around that Lawrence was one of the men coming toward the school. But to her horror one of the men was Russell Dalton, the detective. "Children behave yourselves, I'll be right back."

Abigail grabbed the baby basket and swung it under her arm and then ran down the hall and poked her head into the midwife's room. "Lene, would you look after little Lawrence for me?"

"Vy yes. I would love to." She patted the baby on the cheek. "Now vee vill take care of him."

After that she bolted for the front door and as soon as she got there she swung it open.

The detective approached her. "Mrs. Armstrong I have come to the school as I promised to interrogate you."

"Yes…I know but this wounded warrior has to be attended to right now. Please take a seat in the parlor and I'll be with you in a minute," she said. Then she pulled Lawrence into the school and down the hall. "I could feel it was you coming down the road." They kissed passionately; they embraced each other, until Lawrence was buried in folds of Abigail's dress. His lips brushed along her cheeks, her ear and her eyes.

"I missed you something awful Abby," he said. "I discovered that trying to find myself had to be with you. You are part of me. You are the lost part of me that I was looking for and didn't realize it."

"You have to pretend that you are just another soldier that the Fitch school is trying to heal. Don't let on that you are my husband," she said. "Did you talk to that man that you came up the walk with?"

"No. He just asked me what I was doing here and I told him that I was going to the school."

"It's too bad that you don't have something wrong with you beside the limp but it'll have to do."

With that Lawrence took his right hand out of his overcoat and saluted her. It was just a nub. "Is this good enough?" He asked. He held it up, and turned it every which way to look at the damage. "You know it's odd but when I was back on the farm I fed a Billy Yank that had the same amputation. I guess I'm lucky; it was just my hand and not my head. Life is whittling me down Abby."

"Oh my darling." She grabbed his arm and kissed the nub where the hand used to be, and then put it up to her cheek. "My poor soldier."

"It's not too bad," he said and then slipped the reminder of his sacrifice for the Cause back in his pocket.

"I thought the war was over the day you came home." She leaned against him and looked deep into his eyes.

"Not in Kentucky, it wasn't."

"I have the greatest news. You have a son." Abigail giggled with excitement and expected Lawrence to jump with joy but he just stood still not saying a word.

"What's wrong?"

"Look at me," he said. "Can you see me behind a plow with just one hand?" He turned away from Abigail and stared into the dark nothingness of the gloomy hallway. "That's the other reason I came to find you. Noah said he would give us a parcel of land to farm that would be our own, if you would only come back with me."

"You want me to give up my work here and go back to the farm? How can I do that?"

"I don't know. That's a decision you have to make for yourself. I can't make it for you. It's too bad we can't fit everything into our lives that we want. Something has to fall by the wayside."

"Yes I know." At that instant the picture of Lawrence, and the baby, and the faces of her students, and the image of the farm swirled around in her mind. The things she cared about the most battled for her attention.

"I'm sorry for acting that way," Lawrence said. "I'm happy that we had a baby. What's his name?"

"It's Lawrence," she said. "Is that okay?"

"Yes that's great." He tipped his head to the ceiling. "But of course, little Lawrence."

"But there's another problem."

"What is it?"

"The detective from town, the one that you came up the walk with, is suspicious about Burton and I can't seem to do or say anything to put him off the scent of the killing."

"Maybe there's something I could do to throw him off the track."

"No. As far as he is concerned you are just a soldier that he met on the road that has come to the school to be healed." After Abigail introduced Lawrence to one of the nurses she went to the parlor to confront the detective.

Chapter 24

The Detective Probes

The detective, Russell Dalton rocked on the rocker in the living room, as he smoked his black crooked stogie and blew the smoke into the fireplace. He still had his dark brown beaver top hat on and still wore his tan overcoat. His wet knee-high boots left little puddles on the rug just under the rocking chair.

"Mrs. Armstrong I'm here as I promised and I'm going to continue my investigation whether you like it or not." He had a sense of calm and ease when he saw her come into the room. He noticed chalk dust on her dress and between her fingers.

She sat in a high backed chair just across from the detective with her legs crossed in front of her when she sat down. "Well constable I'm here. What do you want?"

He talked in a steady low pitched confident voice, and noticed that she put her hands up to her face, which said to him that she had something to hide.

"You knew him."

"Who?" Abigail asked and then looked down at the floor.

"The dead soldier that we found."

"Oh, he was a soldier?"

"You know perfectly well that he was a soldier. He had your locket on him. How else would he have gotten it if he didn't know you?"

"He stole it." Abigail got up and walked over to the window.

The detective could feel the excitement of the chase and knew he was close to having the truth revealed. He got up out of the chair, like a bloodhound, and smelled the scent of his guilty prey as she huddled in the corner. "We both know that he wasn't a very nice man." He got close to her back, and very close to her right ear. "Then you did know him?" He barked.

"No, I told you I didn't know him." Abigail looked over her shoulder, startled by how close he was to her and moved away from him and nearer to the sofa.

"That's not what your father, Noah told me." He took a step closer to her to see what reaction she had to his accusation.

"He said I knew him?" Abigail grabbed the arms of the couch for support so as not to faint.

"Yes…he said you knew him well. So well, that he understood how you would have given him the locket as a keepsake."

"No…no that's not true. How could he say that? I only knew him as a friend and sergeant to my husband."

The detective's lips smiled around his cigar and then he plucked it out of his mouth and threw it in the fireplace in triumph. "That's what I thought," he said. "You know, they still hang women for capital crimes. Let me see." He stroked his chin and looked up at the ceiling while he tried to remember. "There was Chipita Rodriguez in sixty-three, and two young ones, Paula Angel only nineteen, in April of sixty-one, and Amy Spain just seventeen in sixty-five." Then he walked closer, to put her off balance with the most recent hanging. "Oh yes, Mary Surratt in sixty-five. She was the co-conspirator in the Lincoln assassination."

Suddenly Abigail fell onto the sofa, buried her head in the cushion and began to cry.

"I'm sorry miss but the law must be satisfied," he said. "It's time to tell the truth." He skulked over her, as if she were a prey ready to be snatched up in his jaws and carried away.

"Well…well what do we have here?" Jonathan's voice split the smugness of the detective like an arrow hitting the center of the bull's eye. In an instant he backed away from the couch and uncrossed his arms.

"I'm Russell Dalton, the constable of New Athens. This young lady is a prime suspect in a murder case." He used his position like a weapon for raining abuse on the young girl.

"Mr. Dalton I'm Jonathan Fitch and she is my client. You should have come to me first so that I could have seen to it that Abigail was represented and protected by me before you started questioning her."

"Oh, I didn't know." The detective shrank away from any confrontation and sat down on the rocking chair because he knew his was out matched.

Jonathan went over to Abigail and sat next to her and pulled her up and off the cushions of the sofa and put her head on his shoulder. "It's all right Abigail he won't bother you anymore."

"He said that they were going to hang me." She sniffled. "Are they?"

"No…don't worry about that. He just said that to scare you."

The constable leaned forward while he still rocked in the chair with his fists clenched and said; "She has to come back with me to New Athens to stand trial."

"That's not going to happen sir. I'm an officer of the court and will take full responsibility for her. Besides, she just gave birth and a long bumpy ride might cause complications. Are you prepared to take on any blame if anything goes wrong?"

The detective stretched his neck and loosened his collar. "No I guess not. But she has to keep herself available."

With Abigail still in his arms he talked to the police officer. "Sometimes justice has to be tempered with mercy. Have you ever read The Merchant of Venice? There, if they followed the letter of the law the man would have been dead and the law would have been fulfilled. We are not going to do that with this woman. You have my word as a lawyer and a gentleman that I will keep my eye on her. Now, if you will excuse me I have to attend to my client."

With his top hat in his hands he headed out of the parlor towards the door. "I'm just doing my job Mr. Fitch. There are too many unanswered questions back there in New Athens and the answers to those questions have led me here. She knows all about what happened and is unwilling to talk about it."

Jonathan just watched as the constable embarrassed, went towards the door.

He moved at a snail's pace, not quite sure what had just happened to his lawbreaker. Should I try to take her by force, should I go back and argue further with her attorney, or should I go back to New Athens and come back with more deputies, he thought. He finally put on his wool gloves and his top hat and pulled hard on the door as he stormed out into the snow.

Chapter 25

Abigail finds Lawrence Again.

She suddenly got up out of his arms and curtsied. "Thank you Mr. Fitch for coming to my rescue." Then she ran back to her unattended classroom. To her surprise all the students had their heads in their McGuffey readers. "For being so good you can all have the rest of the afternoon off."

They just sat there for a second not realizing what their teacher had just said. A universal thank you welled up from the crowd of students; "Thank you so very much Miss Armstrong."

The classroom was emptied in a flash. All the rows of students bumped and shuffled against each other until all that was left were vacant desks that stared at the ceiling and little Lawrence as he gazed up at Abigail.

Abigail's insides were about to burst, she was so anxious to see Lawrence. He was so close yet so far. Their rendezvous had to be secret, and that diminished the time she could have with him but not the passion she felt.

She grabbed Little Lawrence and made for Lene's room. The midwife sat on her bed listing to one side, about to fall asleep.

"Lene!" Would you take care of the baby for a while longer?"

She turned her head towards the door, blinked her eyes and frowned. "Oh…Abigail vat is the matter? You vant me to watch the baby?"

"Yes, please."

"Now vee vill watch the baby. Go…go do vat you need to do."

She went outside, headed for the hospital and in the direction of the medical wing.

The annex was long and white with beds that had white linen sheets and pillows on them. The pillows were big and round and the sheets were neatly tucked under the mattresses. Each bed looked like a fluffy cloud.

"I'm looking for the soldier that came in recently with the amputated right hand and a limp," she said to the nurse that stood at the entrance to the ward.

The nurse had kind blue eyes and pointed to a bed in the middle of the ward.

Her legs shook as she tried very much to make it seem that she was just going to visit a stranger, a fallen soldier, a casualty of the war. But her breath quickened and her heart jumped when she saw Lawrence asleep on his bunk. She stood at the foot of his bed and wanted to jump into the bed with him but she held herself in check with all the strength that she could muster. She imagined herself as she jumped into the bunk and cuddle up to his side to feel the warmth of his body against hers.

She grabbed the foot of the bed and shook it gently. "Soldier…soldier I've come to see if you're feeling better?" Then she just stood there with her hands folded in front of her.

Lawrence turned his head in her direction, wiped his forehead with the nub and blinked his eyes. "Wha…Oh it's you miss Abigail." He looked around to make sure that nobody heard what they said to each other. "Thank you for visiting me." Then he whispered; "meet me down the hall in the pantry."

Every soldier's head turned and watched Abigail walk pass them. She could feel their eyes watch her leave the room. As soon as she got out of the ward, she scrunched against the wall and waited for the instant that Lawrence passed by.

The small food cupboard was cozy and familiar to Abigail. The light from the barracks cast a soft bluish glow to the small space.

All of a sudden two girls and two boys broke through the romantic silence. The girls giggled and squealed as they scamper by. "Children!" Abigail hollered. "This is no place to run around. There's men here that are very sick not only in their bodies but in their minds too."

They skidded to a stop and stared into the darkness surprised that Abigail was in the shadows. "Sorry ma'am," the tall boy said. "We'll be quieter." Then they left through a small door that was attached to the scullery. Abigail was happy when she noticed that they were somebody else's students. After all, she had let her class out sooner than they expected and the thought of them running all over the school made her nervous.

Even before Lawrence reached the pantry Abigail could smell his body. It brought back the scent of new mown hay and the aroma of sweet leather. Suddenly he was on top of her buried in the folds of her dress. Not a word was said; they just stood and embraced each other and kissed passionately. Now Abigail felt complete.

He reached into his pocket with his good left hand and came out with his mother's ring, which he had put on her finger long ago. "Here," he said as he slipped the ring back on her finger. "It seems that we've been in this situation once before." He looked at the dishes and the table linens piled up on the shelves of the pantry.

"Oh… Lawrence, your mother's ring." She held it against the subdued light while it sparkled in her eyes. She knew then that they were attached forever.

"It's only right that you should wear the ring again since we've found each other again. Don't you think?"

"Yes, yes." Then she hugged him.

He got a faraway look in his eyes and then whispered in her ear; "Kentucky was beautiful Abby. I can still see the image of the horses, big and brown, black and wild and how they ran through their pastures like Pegasus as he flew through the sky. Their muscle's tensed when they walked and rippled when they ran. The blue grass fed those magnificent animals and they were cherished by their owners. But the owners of the farms treated their slaves just as they had always treated them, as nothing but property and investments not as human beings."

"Is that why you came back?"

"It's possible that was some of the reason, but despite that fact there was still a war going on there. I felt that I could only complete myself with you by my side."

"I'm so glad you came home Lawrence." She suddenly backed away. "I love three things in this world; I love you, I love little Lawrence and I love being a teacher. How can I keep all three?"

"I don't know." He pulled her close and cradled her head on his shoulder.

Everything seemed to be the way it was meant to be. Abigail was content now that she had Lawrence back with her and had a new baby to share with him.

Chapter 26

Death Stalks Abigail

Without warning a shot rang out from down the hall, in the direction of Elizabeth's classroom. Soon after that screams echoed through the building and people hollered at each other with the sound of panic in their voices.

"Lawrence what could that be?" Abigail held onto the jam of the door and peeked around the corner.

"That was definitely a gun shot. Sounded like the shot from a pistol." Lawrence took cautious steps out into the hallway as Abigail followed close behind.

Constance barred their way; "There's a madman with a gun in Elizabeth's classroom," Constance said. "He shot somebody but we're not sure who."

Lawrence inched his way past Constance and close to the door of the class, and glanced into the room. "There's a soldier in there sittin' on a desk with a pistol in his hand and all the kids are huddled in a group at the back of the class. I think the teacher is shot. She's lying on the floor."

Abigail whispered in Lawrence's ear; "The nightmare continues." To everybody's surprise Abigail made a run for the classroom. As soon as she got in she kneeled down next to Elizabeth. Without any concern for the killer, she tried to lift Elizabeth up off the floor. "You can't die. You're the only friend I've got," she screamed.

"Abigail get out of there," Lawrence pleaded.

Abigail held Elizabeth in her arms and rocked back and forth as if she were a baby that needed to be comforted. All of a sudden she dropped her friend's lifeless body and ran at the murderer. "No…no, I won't let this happen again." She grabbed the gun out of his hand and pointed it at him. To her surprise the tall muscular soldier dropped his head on one of the desks and began to sob.

Lawrence walked into the room and at once took the gun out of her hand. "It's over Abby."

"Just like Burton," she said. "Are we cursed?"

"No." He held her in his arms as she began to cry on his chest.

"Abigail, who is this man?" Constance asked.

Her muffled voice talked into Lawrence's shirt. "My husband." Then she turned her head and stared at Elizabeth. "My poor friend. She had the misfortune to inherit the burden of my curse."

Lawrence stared at Elizabeth too. "Such a beautiful woman. She must have had plans to get married and have children."

"Yes she did. Now that's all gone," Abigail said.

"Now that she's dead I wonder what the purpose of her life was. What was it that she could have accomplished if not killed? Who knows what great things could have been accomplished if she were still alive."

Abigail raised her voice in frustration. "She was supposed to be a teacher. She was supposed to teach, that was her purpose."

"Sometimes I feel like a puppet on a string Abby, as if I were being directed to do things that I don't want to do, just like that soldier over there." He nodded at the killer. "I want so much to do the right thing."

"And the right thing is to own up to what happened on the farm last summer." She looked up into Lawrence's face. The death of her friend welled up in her the desire to fix the world, or just her piece of it, so these tragic things were less likely to occur.

All of a sudden Lawrence realized what he said. "Yes Abigail, you're right. It's time to unbury Burton."

By this time the students had milled around the dead body, they cried and hugged each other as they looked at their dead teacher. Some of the children stole glances at the soldier that was slumped over the small student desk. He gripped hard onto the desk and breathed heavy into the surface of the small table.

Lawrence walked over to the man and as he did, he continued to point the gun at him for safety; "Why did you do this brother?" Lawrence asked as he used the barrel of the gun as a pointer.

He slowly lifted his head, and with blood shot eyes looked straight at Lawrence. "I couldn't help myself. Do you understand what I'm saying? I couldn't help it." Then he dropped his head back down on the writing table with a thud.

"Yes I understand," he said. He turned to Constance. "You better get the Sherriff so he can put this fella' in a cell."

Constance grabbed one of the boys and told him to go get the constable that lived down the street in one of the houses that faced the school "But where down the road?" The boy asked.

"Oh never mind, I'll go myself," Constance said. She ran out the door and in the direction of a white colonial house across the street. Abigail followed her to the door and watched as she ran down the path and towards the house.

It seemed to Abigail that it looked like a house that a policeman would live in; the bottom porch had four white pillars that supported it which she saw as bars in a giant cell, the second floor had a high peaked roof that resembled the high top wide brimmed hat that sheriff's wore, and the door and the shutters convinced her even more that the man that would be dragged across the street was to be feared, because the door was blood red and the windows were edged with black shutters.

Constance came out the front door with the constable in tow. He only just had one arm in the sleeve of his jacket as he struggled to put his other arm in the other sleeve as she pulled him down his walkway and into the road. A minute later they were in the classroom.

Abigail pulled Lawrence away from all the commotion. "I can't take anymore of this. Let's go."

"You don't want to see what happens?"

"No. I can't stand seeing Elizabeth lying there dead on the floor."

"Okay let's get out of here."

Chapter 26

The Smell of Eagerness

The gruesome details of moving the dead body, and the questions asked of the soldier that was put in irons and moved to the jail went on without delay. The classes that would have taken place were put on hold until the black mist of the murder faded away and seeped out and through the walls of the school.

The next day while Lawrence and Abigail and the baby were having breakfast one of the students came up to them and said; "Miss Armstrong we would like to show you something that we thought up. It's a little surprise." The girl shifted from one foot to the other and her chin dipped down against her chest.

"Okay let's go," Abigail said. She positioned the baby basket under her arm and the three of them followed the student into the auditorium.

The pungent smell of glue, construction paper and the waxy odor of crayons filled the large room.

Little Lawrence began to cry so Abigail put a bottle in his mouth. After he sucked on the bottle for a short while, he dozed off to the baby world of dreams.

"Is he asleep?" Lawrence asked and then leaned in front of Abigail to get a look at the baby. "You couldn't wake him up if you fired cannons next to his ear."

Abigail laughed and then smiled down at baby Lawrence.

In the back of the stage were canvases with painted scenes of mountains, rivers and a blue sky above them. Around the top and sides of the stage were painted images of tall green pine trees. The children wanted to give the illusion of being in the wilderness that Lewis and Clark had explored.

A little girl with blonde pigtails and dressed in buckskins came out on the stage holding a picture of Sacajawea; "This is Sacajawea and this is her story." Then she disappeared into the wing of the stage.

Two boys came out, one dressed in buckskins and a coonskin hat and the other one with a three cornered hat and colonial clothes on.

The boy with the three cornered hat said; "Hello, my name is Meriwether Lewis and I was the scientist and the leader of the forty men in three boats that went up the Missouri River." He bowed down and with his hat in his hand he made a wide sweep of his arm and gestured to the side of the stage. There, where he had pointed was a picture of three flat bottom boats drawn on a large piece of colored paper.

Abigail buried her face in Lawrence's arm and tried not to laugh. "Oh Lawrence they are so serious about their play. I can't laugh, it'll hurt their feelings," she said. "Aren't they cute?"

"They sure are." He smiled.

Then the next boy came forward. "I'm William Clark and was considered the pathfinder along with Sacajawea." He removed his coonskin cap and held it over his chest.

Thomas Jefferson came on stage and faced the audience. "These two explorers along with Sacajawea found a way to the Pacific ocean. I had to open up the wilderness after purchasing The Louisiana Purchase."

Thomas Jefferson left the stage at the same time that Sacajawea came onto it. A tall girl, as tall as the boys, dressed in Indian skins and with a papoose carrier on her back and wearing moccasins walked into the middle of the stage. "I am Sacajawea and I led Lewis and Clark through the wilderness." She turned her head and looked at baby carrier. "This is Jean Baptiste my son that I carried with me." The doll's head bobbed around the carrier when she glanced back.

Abigail bent over and put her face in her hands and tried very much not to laugh. "I can't help it. They're so cute and they've tried so hard to present a real play but it's tickling my funny bone."

Lawrence rubbed her back. "You have to be in control. Like you said, you don't want to hurt their feelings."

She sat up all of a sudden with a straight back against the chair. "Yes you're right." Although she still had a slight smile on her face and was trying hard not to laugh.

Then a canoe was brought out on stage with a load crash. The three students got in it. Lewis and Clark sat on both ends with paddles in their hands and Sacajawea sat in the middle.

A student came on stage and took Jean Baptiste, (the doll), off her back and carried it off stage.

Suddenly the canoe capsized and they all fell out. Sacajawea stood up with a journal and a sack of flour in her hand as Lewis and Clark sat on the stage and looked up at the Indian girl.

She held up the items and said; "These were the only supplies that we had and I rescued them. Not only that but I saved the surveying instruments and other equipment by diving to the bottom of the river and coming up with things that mapped the land."

All of a sudden thirty students came onto the stage dressed as Indians. The chief spoke; "I am the chief of the Shoshoni tribe and you are welcome to stay at our camp because Sacajawea is my sister and has a baby that has to be taken care of."

With that, all the students sat down in a large crescent while they faced the audience.

Then the same little girl with the blonde pigtails came back out onto the stage with a script in her hands and started to read from it. "The reason that Sacajawea and Lewis and Clark were so successful meeting the Indians was because they were not seen as a threat, after all they were just two white men and a young Indian girl with a papoose."

She sat down and Sacajawea got up; "I knew that first day when I first met Lewis and Clark that I would die any time to save their lives."

Abigail stopped her smile and stared at the students on the stage. She realized that they had captured the true meaning of Sacajawea's journey. Abigail rushed up the stairs and onto the stage and she hugged every student that she could wrap her arms around.

Tears of joy streamed down her cheeks. "That was wonderful children."

A little boy dressed in buckskin shouted out from the back of the crowd. "This play was for you Miss Armstrong."

Abigail turned to Lawrence. "See, this is why I'm going to have a hard time going back to the farm," she said. "If only I could have both then I would be supremely happy."

"I understand what you're saying Abby. I wish there was something I could do about that." Then he got up with little Lawrence under his arm, placed the basket on the boards and leaned over the front of the stage as he looked at all the students dressed in their costumes.

While Abigail stood there her face went pale and her knees started to buckle. In the back of the auditorium was the detective Russell Dalton, and what looked like two deputies, and they were standing tall and defiant against the wall as they stared at her.

The deputies, one in a Union army shirt and pants, and the other in a farmer's overalls and a Scottish hat tipped to the side of his head stared at Abigail.

"Miss Armstrong I have a warrant for your arrest." The constable waved the document over his head. As the paper made a crackle above his skull she became queasy while she thought about the fact that it was a death warrant.

Everybody froze with terror and disbelief. "I'm Lawrence Ellsworth. Abigail's husband. If there is anything legal that has to be attended to then we had better have our lawyer present, he shouted." He patted Abigail on the face and smiled. "Don't worry Abby I'll go get Jonathan."

He clunked down the steps and dashed off to get their lawyer.

"Why don't you leave me alone Mr. Dalton?" With that, the children assembled around her like a protective cocoon. Every child's heart became like the heart of a lion and they were determined that this stranger was not going to take their hero away without a fight.

" You're guilty and I intend to prove it." He stalked closer to the stage. "Now that your Husband is here we'll be able to get to the bottom of it."

The sound of chairs being pushed aside and the scuffle of feet on the wood floor sliced through the tension in the hall.

Jonathan Fitch entered the room with Lawrence just behind him. "I told you constable Dalton that you have to see me first before you can interrogate my client."

"Not if I have this," he said. He waved the warrant in the air again.

Jonathan paced over to the detective and snatched the document out of his hand. He unfolded it and read it with a lawyer's passion for the welfare of his client and tried to find some loop-hole out of the warrant.

He dropped the papers to his side and with a sad face and turned towards the couple. "I'm sorry folks. This seems all in order to me. You'll have to go with the detective back to New Athens."

Chapter 27

The Steps up to the Gallows

That afternoon, after Abigail had pried herself away from her precious students, she had tears in her eyes. The memory of them as they pulled at her dress and tried to hold her back from her departure made her reluctant to go but she had no choice.

It was a bitter sweet exodus; the friendship of Elizabeth and then the bitterness of her murder, the alliance of Constance and then the betrayal later on, the joy of being a teacher only to be yanked away by the Burton curse, and then the final bitterness of all, in having to go back to stand trial for defending herself against a madman.

The stagecoach was already packed under orders from Constance. She stood in the window of the school and watched Abigail, Lawrence and the baby load into the cramped coach with a self-satisfied smirk on her face.

In contrast to Constance, the children congregated around the windows of the school. They were still dressed in their costumes with their faces pressed hard against the panes of glass, as all sixty students pushed and shoved to get a better look at Abigail as she left.

Somewhere in their young hearts they knew that the days of curious questions about how the world worked were over. They had to settle for 'that's just the way it is.'

In the stagecoach, the family sat on one set of seats across from the sheriff flanked by his deputies. All the way to New Athens, Russell Dalton kept an eagle eye on their every movement, even while the couple slept.

At last, after a day and a half of travel, and around noon, the coach pulled up in front of Wilson's Farm. The farm hadn't changed except for the fact that there were bales of hay piled up on the lawn waiting to be loaded onto a hay wagon and transported into town.

"Why did you bring me here?" Abigail asked. "This isn't my home anymore."

"It's so I can keep an eye on you and everybody else connected to the case." He opened the stagecoach door. "Okay, get out and don't leave the farm." The springs squeaked as the family got out of the coach.

They stood there while the carriage turned in the road and headed for town. The chains on the harnesses jingled and a horse neighed as the carriage disappeared down the road behind a cloud of dust.

The three men that were the most important to Abigail, except for Lawrence, stepped out from behind the ten foot high bales of hay.

William and Daniel approached her first. "Good afternoon Miss Abigail," Daniel said.

"Hey Daniel." With that, she hiked up little Lawrence closer to her side so as not to drop the baby basket.

Then William walked up to Lawrence. He shook his hand. "Glad to see that you brought back Abigail."

"We didn't have much choice about coming back," Lawrence said as he dropped William's hand.

Not knowing what to say to Abigail, William said the first thing that came to his mind. "Are you still lookin' at the moon with the telescope?"

"Yes. I can't get enough of looking at it. It seems so different from the earth."

They both smiled and then there was a long pause as Noah walked up to Abigail.

All the men stood as if they were frozen in place unable to move or react to the situation.

"Hi Pa."

Noah didn't say a word. He just caressed Abigail's cheek with the back of his hand, kissed the baby on its bald forehead, and put his arm around her shoulder as they walked up to the summer kitchen together. It was the first time since they closed the kitchen for the winter that it was going to be opened.

When they got to the kitchen Noah started to make coffee. "Everybody sit down and make yourself comfortable. I'll make the java."

All at once Little Lawrence began to cry. Without any hesitation Abigail got a bottle from the Haversack that Lawrence had placed on the floor. She placed the bottle in the baby's mouth.

The shuffle of Noah's boots and the clang of the tin pot and tin cups rang out above the movement of everybody as they got settled in their chairs.

Both Daniel and William raised their eyebrows and snickered when they saw Noah serve the coffee like a common housemaid. Noah stood and leaned against the sink as he drank his black coffee. William and Daniel sat across from each other and Abigail sat on Lawrence's lap with the baby in a white basket asleep next to her under the table.

By now everybody had a steaming cup of coffee in front of them when Abigail broke the silence. "Do you remember when we were kids and it was your first day on the farm and we met up with the bear Cleopatra?"

Lawrence stared into his coffee cup. "Yeah. I was so scared of that bear. And she was so fat from eating all those blueberries and apples."

"Me too. That same terror I felt in the pit of my stomach I feel now because of this Burton thing."

"Yes I know what you're saying Abigail. It seems everything has fallen apart," Lawrence said. "The only good thing is that we're home now and safe on the farm."

Abigail turned to Noah. "Is that true Pa? Are we safe and at home?"

"Yes Abby you're safe and at home." They smiled at each other and then sipped on their coffee.

"I wish Jonathan was here. He seemed like he knew what to do." She stole a glance at Lawrence and he nodded.

"Who's that?" Noah asked.

"He was a lawyer that helped me at the Fisk school."

"We have to be at the courthouse at eight in the morning tomorrow," Noah said.

"It seems we is always givin' help and gettin' nothing back," Daniel said. Then he shook his head as he looked down at the floor.

"I can really pity the guy that gives and gets nothing in return," William said. "When I was younger I worked as a chimney sweep and all I got for my trouble was a cold bed on top of a coal sack. We've all come a long way. We can't give up now, we have to fight."

"But how?" Abigail asked.

"I don't know yet but I think something will happen that will show us the way to get out of this mess."

The rest of the afternoon the men loaded the hay wagons and brought them into town to sell the hay while Abigail worked in the kitchen making a roast chicken, roasted potatoes and yellow squash for dinner.

After they delivered their cargo they stopped in the bar and drank so many beers that they lost count. They leaned on the bar and filled their bellies so their heads would become empty, and forget about the court date the next morning. For that matter they staggered out the door and bobbed and weaved on the seats of their wagons as they focused on the whirling road ahead of them. It turned out that even Noah with all his experience driving a hay wagon, drove it into the ditch three times.

When they got home everybody just left the horses still harnessed and tied to the stalls in the barn. Supper would go to waste because all the 'Kings Men' were dead drunk.

Abigail walked into the barn and chuckled and shook her head. "I guess they're entitled," she whispered.

As it happened, it became an early night. Abigail retired to her room upstairs, the room that Noah kept just the same, in hopes she would someday return, just as she had kept the root cellar the same in anticipation of Lawrence's return.

She fell asleep on her feather bed with her arm draped over the side as she clenched the handle of the baby basket in her left hand. Ever since she had gotten home she had a terror deep in her heart that she would wake one morning and discover the baby gone.

The nightmare she had that night only made her more fearful. She dreamed that Burton was alive and that she could hear the thump of his boots as he stalked up the stairs towards her bedroom. He entered the room, drew his gun and shot Little Lawrence. The white wicker basket turned red with blood. After that he banged on the wall with the broken courting stick. All of a sudden she woke up and realized that it was a nightmare, even though it seemed so real. But the knock was from the door downstairs.

The baby was safe. Just before she peered over the side of the bed she got a whiff of the clean linens in and around little Lawrence, it was then she knew it was a dream. When she picked up the wicker basket and slipped it through her arm it creaked and protested being roused in the middle of the night.

Her tiny feet pointed at the risers with great care as she tip-toed down the stairs toward the front entrance; the pendulum clock chimed three times as she opened the heavy door. "Jonathan. What are you doing here?" She set the baby down. She lit an oil lamp and lifted it high above her head.

"I 've come to help you with the trial," he said. "You do need help don't you?"

The flame in the lamp hissed and shed a flickering glow to the room.

"Oh yes. You're an answer to a prayer. Please come in."

He scraped the mud off the bottom of his boots before he came into the living room. Then he removed his top hat and put it on the couch.

"I knew you had to go with the constable after he showed me the papers but you were hustled out of the school so fast that I didn't have a chance to tell you that I would still be representing you."

"You can stay in Noah's room for now until we can get you settled in more permanently."

"Thank you Abigail. That would be just fine."

He picked up his hat from the sofa and as he reached the middle of the stairs Abigail said; "I'm afraid of what might happen to me and my new family if it doesn't go well in court."

He turned and looked at her with a furrowed brow. "I have some things that I'll bring up at the trial that might get you released from any further prosecution." Then he went upstairs.

Chapter 28

Who's Guilty?

Abigail, Lawrence and the baby were on one side of the room, behind a large table, with Jonathan next to them with his briefcase open in front of him with papers on top of it.

The other side of the room had the prosecutor for the county, with his chair pushed back so it leaned on the railing and a large cigar between his fingers. He looked self assured and seemed confident that the case was already decided.

The gallery had a few curious strangers in it along with Daniel, William and Noah.

Russell Dalton was up near the judge. He bent forward close to his ear as they talked. The judge had a strong posture, with his shoulders back, chest out, chin high and a permanent smirk on his face.

Lawrence leaned towards Jonathan. "Russell seems awful friendly with the judge. Don't you think?"

"He should be. Russell is his nephew."

"Oh no…we're doomed."

"Don't worry so much. They may be relatives but they're not above the law."

"Mr. Fitch are you ready to proceed?" the judge asked.

Jonathan got up from his seat. "Yes your honor."

"Mr. Creedmoor are you ready?" The prosecutor's chair flopped back onto the floor and then he placed his cigar in the ashtray straightened his suit and stood as if at attention.

"Yes judge. The state is ready."

"Proceed."

"The state calls Russell Dalton to the stand." The detective walked up to the leather chair with poise and assurance as he took wide steps and winked at the judge when he sat down. "Can you point out to the court the woman you suspect of killing the soldier you found?"

"Right over there."—He pointed at Abigail—"She admitted to me that she killed him."

"And you told me that you felt she was sorry for the killing but there was nothing she could do?"

"I object your honor." Jonathan stood up quick.

"Yes." The judge leaned forward.

"How could he know how my client felt at the time of the killing?"

"Sustained."

"Let me rephrase that question. What did she say about the broach that you found on the body?"

"She doubted that Noah, her father gave him the locket."

The prosecutor leaned into Russell. "Then she did admit that it was hers?"

"Yes."

"That's all. Thank you Mr. Dalton." Then the lawyer sat down and Jonathan got up.

"What did she say about her fear of Burton?"

"I don't know what you mean."

"Did she say that she was afraid that he would try to kill her too?"

Russell fidgeted in the chair. "I don't remember."

Jonathan turned to the judge. "Your honor please instruct the witness to answer the question."

The judge's chair squeaked as he tilted towards the detective. "You have to answer the question."

"In that case."—he squirmed in his chair again before he answered—"Yes, she did say she was afraid of being killed by him."

"That's all. No more questions at this time. The witness is excused." Russell walked past the defendants with a cynical smile before he sat down.

The prosecutor got up. "At this time I'd like to call Lawrence Ellsworth to the stand."

As Lawrence got up to go to the witness box Abigail grabbed his arm. He bent down. "It's all right Abby. I'll be okay." Then he went over and sat down on the witness chair.

He sat straight and confident. "Now, tell the court in your own words what transpired that day." The prosecutor went over and sat on the edge of the table as he listened to the testimony.

"Well there's not much to tell. Burton came down the stairs while he waved his gun in the air. He fired it once as he came down the stairs."

"At you?"

"I'm not sure. The shot split the courting stick that we found, in half. When he got down the stairs I wacked the pistol out of his hand with a fireplace poker."

"Is that when Abigail shot him?"

"No… she never shot him. It was me."

Jonathan at once stood up. "Your honor can I have a moment to confer with my client?"

"No Jonathan it's all right," Lawrence said. "Please sit down."

"Okay." Jonathan sat down, put his head on the table and covered his head with his arms.

"Then it was you that shot the soldier?" the prosecutor asked.

Before he could answer, Abigail stood up. "It was me," she shouted.

The judge slammed the gavel. "Order in the court."

After that, Lawrence was excused from the witness chair and Abigail was summoned to the stand. She looked ready to testify as she leaned forward and looked into the eyes of the lawyer.

"It's evident that your husband lied to protect you," the prosecutor said. "Will you tell us the truth now?"

"Yes." She said. "When Lawrence knocked the gun out of his hand, I picked it up and shot him."

"Thank you Mrs. Ellsworth. I think that settles that question." Then the lawyer walked over to his table and sat down.

Jonathan popped up from the defendant table and went over to Abigail.

"First of all Abigail can you tell me what you felt at that moment. The moment the gun was in your hand and you fired it at Burton?"

"I was scared he would kill Lawrence."

"Is that all you felt at that moment?"

"No. I was scared he was going to kill me too."

"Then what you're saying is that you felt that you had no choice?" Jonathan walked over to the table and sat on the edge of it and looked over at the prosecutor. "Your witness."

The prosecutor looked at the floor, and when he approached Abigail, he all of a sudden looked up at her and then bent over close to her face. "Was he armed?"

"No of course not. I already told you I had his gun."

"Then you shot an unarmed man in the back?"

Jonathan got up quick. "Abigail you don't have to answer that."

"He was going to kill Lawrence," Abigail said at once.

"Your honor. The witness has the right not to incriminate herself." Jonathan leaned on his palms as he stretched his neck towards his honor.

"Sustained," the judge said.

"That's all," the prosecutor blurted out. "The state rests."

"The defense has no more witnesses. But I would like to address your honor with a further argument that I would like you to consider."

"Proceed," the judge said as he leaned back in his leather high back chair.

"Self-defense. It is a fundamental human right. To protect ourselves and our home is at the core of everything that we hold dear in this country. That is what this young lady was doing. She was protecting herself and her loved one. I can't see how this court can come to any other conclusion but for acquittal." Then Jonathan sat back down at the defense table, and as he did he patted Lawrence's and Abigail's shoulders to reassure them.

"Thank you Mr. Fitch," The judge said. "Since you elected to have this criminal case tried by me without a jury I will let you know by tomorrow at ten in the morning what my decision will be."

Chapter 29

Daniel Saves Abigail

After the trial everybody went back home, to Noah's farm. They all ended up in the summer kitchen. This place was where the problems of the world were solved, the place where the heart and mind felt free, and the place where all their questions seemed to be answered over a hot cup of coffee. Like the gods of Olympus, their black steaming ambrosia seemed to make everything right.

"So what do you think?" Noah asked Jonathan.

"It doesn't look good. I think we have to prepare ourselves for the worst."

"What do you mean?" Abigail asked.

"There might be some jail time to serve."

"Oh no…" She buried her head in Lawrence's chest and began to cry.

Jonathan looked away at the floor and began to sweat. "I'm going to take a walk." But before leaving the kitchen he turned around and said; "Rest, Abigail. We have a long day ahead of us tomorrow." He went out the door, and headed for the fields in back of the house. That was the last the group saw him until later that afternoon.

"What's the matter with Jonathan?" William asked.

"I think he's come to the end of his rope and he feels bad about not doing more to help us." Lawrence said.

After that Abigail was tired and flopped on the sofa in the living room.

After she had fallen asleep Noah lit his pipe and stared at her through the smoke that rose from the bowl. "Look at Abigail. She seems so peaceful and content lying there. She looks like a corpse with her hands laced together over her chest. Not a care in the world. Better she were dead than to have to go through this."

"Pa," Lawrence said. "You don't mean that?"

"No, of course not. It just seems so hopeless." He snuffed out the red hot ember in the bowl of his pipe with his thumb and without as much as a frown of pain on his brow.

"Mista Noah, I got an idea that will fix everthin," Daniel said.

"Not now Daniel. We have to think what to do. Now please hush up."

There was a painful silence in the room that was broken up by the shuffle of their boots on the wooden floor and the occasional sip of coffee.

At long last Lawrence looked up from the table at Daniel. "What's your idea?" At this point Lawrence was so desperate, that anything even in the least possible was a welcome idea.

Daniel could see that Noah was annoyed with him when he stepped forward because he looked at him with raised eyebrows and a glassy stare.

"Well here it is. As I sees it, if Abigail was dead then there would be nobody to send to jail."

"This is no time for nonsense," Noah said. He walked in front of Daniel and pushed him aside to get to the coffee pot.

"Pa, listen to what he has to say," Lawrence said.

"Oh all right." He leaned back on the sink and took small sips of coffee as he listened.

"You remember me tellin' you about Mother Cleo and magic she gave us to cure my sister?"

"Yes I remember Daniel," Lawrence said. "Yes, yes what are you driving at?"

"She has a potion that makes it look like you is dead."

"Go get it."

Daniel jumped up from his chair and ran up the stairs as if he were being chased by a posse of barking dogs. There was the sound of drawers being opened up and the shuffle of furniture being pushed around that echoed through the room.

He plucked a small smoky colored vial from the back of the drawer and put it in his pocket and then ran down the stairs back into the summer kitchen.

"Here it is." He held it out in the palm of his hand.

Lawrence got up and walked over and looked down at the bottle as if it were sacred holy water that had to be respected and at the same time feared. He picked it up with care, with his thumb and pointing finger.

He held it up to the light. "So this is it."

"Yes'um."

"Abigail wake up." Lawrence went over to the sofa where Abigail was sleeping and nudged her shoulder. "We have a solution to our problem."

"Wha…what's the matter?"

"Daniel has a potion that will make it appear that you have died." He held it up in front of her.

She grabbed the bottle and cradled it against her chest. "The answer to a prayer. What do I do?"

Lawrence looked at Daniel

"Just put it in some milk or somethin' and drink it down." Daniel's eyes were sad but hopeful.

Lawrence got a glass of milk from the ice box and everybody watched as he took the vial from Abigail and poured the potion into the glass.

"Are you sure you want to do this?" Lawrence asked Abigail.

"Of course. I trust Daniel with my life.

She drank it fast as she looked over the rim of the glass at Daniel. Then she lay down and appeared to fall asleep.

After a while Noah came over and lifted her head up and stared into her face. "You devil. She's dead."

Noah got up and grabbed Daniel by the throat and backed him against the wall. "You killed her."

Lawrence came between them and said; "Put a mirror to her nose. That'll tell us if she's gone or not."

Lawrence put the mirror to her nose and saw the life giving breath fog up the mirror. "See, she's still with us." He held the mirror in his hand and pointed it at the crowd.

"Hurry up go get the doctor from town. If he declares her dead then we're in the clear."

William hopped on a horse and went to town. After ten minutes he came back with Dr. Andrew Taylor. He had a burley mustache and piercing blue eyes, and wire-rimmed glasses on.

As soon as he came through the door he popped open his little black bag and put on his stethoscope. He put it up to her chest and then settled it on the carotid artery in her neck. He was the new doctor in town and wanted to make a good impression, so he made it seem that he knew more than he did so that the new neighborhood would accept him without question.

He turned to Lawrence. "This young lady is dead."

"Are you sure?"

"Absolutely sure." He folded his scope as it coiled around his wrist like a rubber snake. He placed it in the black bag. "I'm sorry."

"How could this happen? She was a young woman, "Lawrence said.

"Was she under any kind of stress lately?"

"Yes. She was just at trial and before that she had her baby."

"I don't know what to tell you. Sometimes these things happen and we don't know why." Just before he left the house he turned to Lawrence. "I'll make out the death certificate. You can come by anytime and pick it up."

"Thanks Doc."

After the doctor left Lawrence picked up Abigail from the couch and turned to Daniel. "Bring in the pine coffin. We'll put her in it so everybody can see that she's dead."

They lay her down in the box in the center of the living room. Then Lawrence kissed her on the forehead. "It's almost over my love." Just then, their lawyer Jonathan came through the summer kitchen and into the living room.

"What's going on?" He asked as he stared at the corpse.

"Her heart just couldn't take it. The doctor was just here and pronounced her dead."

"All this took place in the short time that I went for a walk?"

"Yes." Lawrence hung his head.

Jonathan draped his arm around Lawrence's shoulder. "I'm sorry that this happened Lawrence. If there's anything I can do don't hesitate to let me know," he said. "I have to go to town now and tell the judge the tragic news."

Jonathan left in his carriage and while he was gone everybody busied themselves as they set up chairs and lit candles around the casket. Wild flowers were place all around the casket and a bouquet of daisies were put at a strategic position just over her chest so that it covered the rise and fall of her chest. The stage was set so that now all they had to do was to relax and let the deception take its course.

Not a half an hour later Jonathan along with the judge and Russell Dalton made an appearance. The judge and the detective walked over near Abigail's head and bent down near her face. "She sure looks dead to me," the Honor said.

"Yep, sure does," Russell said.

"Then these proceedings are over?" Jonathan asked.

"Yes, the case against Abigail Ellsworth is dismissed." The judged said. The detective and the judge left as quickly as they had appeared.

Jonathan hung around next to the casket and stole glimpses at the young teacher that he had lost. "I wasn't much help." He plucked one of the wild flowers from the edge of the coffin and rested it on Abigail's chest. "Rest in peace Abby."

"Thanks Jonathan. We'll never forget what you tried to do," Noah said.

"You know when I put the flowers on her chest I could've sworn I saw her chest move."

"Oh no Jonathan. That's just an optical illusion. I thought I saw the same thing happen," Lawrence said.

"Let me leave you with a lawyer's observation."

"Yes what is it?"

"We as lawyers are supposed to deal in facts not supposition. If something appears to be one way, it's not our job to say that it's anything but what it appears to be. Do you understand what I'm getting at?"

"Yes."

"So long." He put on his hat and flicked the brim with his finger. "Justice has been served." Then he left. Abigail and Lawrence would never see him again.

Chapter 31

The Ellsworth Farm

"Abigail wake up," Lawrence said. Then he wet a rag and rung it out and swabbed her face with it.

She sat up and waved her arms into the air as if she were fighting off an attacker. Her eyes opened and she looked at the flowers in the casket and pushed them aside. She fluttered her eyes as she tried to focus. Her face felt wet and clammy. "Wha…what's happening?"

"It's over. We're free. The trick worked and we can live our lives and don't have to worry about the Burton curse anymore."

"Get me out of here Lawrence." She held her arms out to him. He picked her up and set her down on her feet. It was as if she were on a boat and was getting her sea legs. She wobbled a bit and then reached for the coffin to steady herself.

"Are you all right?"

"I'm okay." She took a deep breath and stood up tall. "That's better."

"Might as well show her the surprise," Noah said.

"What surprise?" Abigail looked to each of the men for an answer but they all smiled and kept quiet. "Isn't anybody going to tell me?"

"No. Let's go for a ride," Lawrence said. After that Lawrence, Abigail and William got in the buckboard and rode past Noah's farm and down the road a couple of miles. After a ten minute ride they rode under a sign that read; 'Double Willow Farm.'

As they passed under the sign Abigail bent backwards in an effort to understand what the sign signified. "What is this place Lawrence?" Then she turned back to William. "William!" William ignored her and just rearranged the blankets around little Lawrence so he didn't have to answer.

The silence built in her chest until a little while later, as they traveled on, a farm house came into view. It was a replica of Noah's farm house except brand new. To the side was a one room building with a bell in the steeple.

Abigail got off the squeaky seat of the carriage and held out her arms in the shape of a cross. "What is this place?"

"It's ours."

"It's ours?" She looked around and then walked over to the small building at the end of the wagon trail. Over the door was a sign. 'Abigail's School House.'

"That's where you can teach; while with the help of William, I can farm the land that your father gave us."

She walked into the building and it smelled like sweet pine and on the blackboard in big letters was; WELCOME MRS. ELLSWORTH. Abigail sat at one of the benches and wept tears of joy.

Lawrence stood in the doorway. "Do you like it Abby?"

"Oh I love it. Thank you Mr. Ellsworth."

"Don't you think that we know each other well enough by now that you can call me Lawrence?" They both laughed as Abigail ran to him and hugged him. He let loose from her hug and she frowned thinking that something was wrong. "Wait; wait till you hear this sound." He walked over to the bell and pulled the rope so that it echoed all over the valley. "Class is officially in session."

"It's so perfect. It's everything I ever wanted; a family, a farm and a career. I feel I'm the luckiest girl alive."

"Life cut us up a bit but we came through it okay now that we have each other."

"Yes." They hugged each other and kissed.

Their days were filled with plowing and planting for Lawrence and William and teaching and maintaining the schoolhouse for Abigail.

Then Lawrence found what he thought was a sacred place. It was an Indian mound that he came across in the forest. It was overgrown with saplings not more than one hundred years old.

He cleared the plateau and planted his most prized corn on top of the mountain. The sun bathed the corn in light from early morning to late dusk, so that the plants grew tall and straight.

Many nights Lawrence and Abigail would lie down in the field and look up at the stars with the spyglass, with little Lawrence in his blanket nearby. For Lawrence it was the fulfillment of a dream. No longer would he fall asleep under the stars alone. No longer would the war dreams plague him. No longer would he have to search for his home, because he was already there.

Then one day Abigail saw that the Burton curse was gone. Russell Dalton rode up to the schoolhouse because he had heard that somebody was teaching but more important to him, was that he had heard that a new schoolmarm was teaching and he had to see for himself if it was Abigail.

She stood on the steps of the building with her arms folded across her chest.

"Yes Mr. Dalton What do you want?"

"I heard there was a new schoolmarm teaching out here at the new Ellsworth farm. Had to see if it was you."

"Well you've seen haven't you?"

"Yes." He reined his horse to the side so he could get a better look at Abigail. "You know that little trick you pulled didn't fool anybody."

"It fooled you didn't it?"

"Yeah I guess you're right."

He pulled up on the reins hard to settle the horse down. He sat there with his elbow on the pommel of the saddle and stared at her without saying a word. Then at long last he said; "Okay you won." He kicked the horse hard in its flanks which made it jump forward as he galloped away down the wagon trail.

The End